'It's twins. I'm expecting twins, Xandros. A [barcode] **of January,' sh**

Twins.

Hot, unwanted emotions washed over him— trying to take him back to a childhood he had buried and forgotten. A mother who had left him. A father who had never been there. A twin brother to whom he was joined for ever—whether he liked it or not. A brother he had fought with. Two men who had allowed time to deepen the rift between them.

He stared at her. 'You are quite sure of this?'

'Yes. They can do a check between nine and—'

'That's enough!' He silenced her with an automatic raise of his hand, the imperious gesture telling her that he was simply not interested in the detail. What the hell did a man do in a situation like this?

'*Say* something!' said Rebecca urgently, because she could bear his brooding silence no longer.

'What do you want me to say, *agape mou*? That we will all live happily ever after and that I will marry you?' He gave a short, bitter laugh. 'Because I have no intention of doing that.'

Modern™ Romance presents a brand-new duet
by star author

SHARON KENDRICK

THE GREEK BILLIONAIRES' BRIDES

*possessed by two Greek billionaire brothers—
as mistresses, as wives…*

Power, pride and passion—divided by bitter rivalry,
discover how only the love and passion of two women
can reunite these wealthy, successful brothers.

Book 1:
THE GREEK TYCOON'S BABY BARGAIN,
on sale May 2008

Book 2:
THE GREEK TYCOON'S CONVENIENT WIFE,
on sale July 2008

THE
GREEK TYCOON'S
BABY BARGAIN

BY
SHARON KENDRICK

MILLS & BOON®
Pure reading pleasure

All the characters in this book have no existence outside the imagination of the author, and have no relation whatsoever to anyone bearing the same name or names. They are not even distantly inspired by any individual known or unknown to the author, and all the incidents are pure invention.

First published in Great Britain 2008
Harlequin Mills & Boon Limited,
Eton House, 18-24 Paradise Road, Richmond, Surrey TW9 1SR

© Sharon Kendrick 2008

ISBN: 978 0 263 86426 7

Set in Times Roman 10½ on 12¼ pt
01-0508-46105

Printed and bound in Spain
by Litografia Rosés, S.A., Barcelona

Sharon Kendrick started story-telling at the age of eleven, and has never really stopped. She likes to write fast-paced, feel-good romances, with heroes who are so sexy they'll make your toes curl! Born in west London, she now lives in the beautiful city of Winchester—where she can see the cathedral from her window (but only if she stands on tiptoe). She has two children, Celia and Patrick, and her passions include music, books, cooking and eating—and drifting off into wonderful daydreams while she works out new plots!

To my adorable godchildren:
Lucy Jacob, Judy Jacob, Hannah Minnock,
Lucy Wightwick, Rory Maguire
and Catriona McDavid. With love.

CHAPTER ONE

IT WASN'T the first time he had been late—but it was the first time he hadn't bothered to warn her.

Outside, the rain made the street look as glossy as an old black and white photo but Rebecca's eyes were fixed at the junction which would give her the first glimpse of his car.

The palms of her hands were cold and clammy and she bit her lip, her head spinning with thoughts she could no longer ignore. Because maybe this was how it all began—the end of a relationship. With the slow, slow drip of inconsideration—rather than the passion of the blazing row.

Her lips curved into a painful smile as she recognised that even calling it a relationship gave it more importance than it deserved. When two people lived on opposite continents and merely snatched at secret moments together—did that really count?

Perhaps *affair* would be more accurate. An affair which should never have started and which she'd tried her best to resist, but in the end she had been weak—of course she had. For wasn't that Xandros's special ability: to make women weak around him? It wasn't difficult to see why. Given the sheer charisma and powerful persuasion of the Greek billionaire, it was amazing that she had lasted out as long as she had.

Maybe this was what happened when you finally began to fall in love with a man like Alexandros Pavlidis—or Xandros to his friends and lovers. This terrible preoccupation which made all your thinking skewed. Even though you told yourself that you didn't want to be in love, that it couldn't possibly *be* love when all you'd known were some amazing dates and some even more amazing sex.

Yet you could tell yourself something again and again and sometimes almost believe it. And then he would call at the very last minute and she would hear that deep sexy voice, asking her if she'd like to have dinner, and her heart would flip—the world seeming suddenly to be lit by fairy lights. And even though she hated herself for being so available, she would be unable to say no.

The gleam of powerful headlights cut a bright channel through the night and Rebecca saw the shiny black nose of the limousine as it slowly eased its way into view. Hastily, she ducked out of sight as it stopped outside the apartment building. Not the most attractive sight in the world, was it? To be seen staring anxiously out of the window!

She checked the mirror. Her hair was clean and shining—worn loose, just the way Xandros liked it. She was wearing a dress in soft lilac and was slim enough and young enough to carry off the relatively inexpensive outfit and make the most of it. Xandros didn't like a lot of make-up and neither did she. A slick of lipstick and a curl of mascara—that was all.

But no amount of careful preparation could hide the faint shadows beneath her eyes, or the way that she seemed to have been constantly biting her lip lately, like an exam candidate who hadn't really understood the question.

The doorbell rang and she pinned a casual smile to her mouth, which died the instant she opened the door to see a tall man in uniform standing on the step, rain dripping from his peaked cap, and it took a moment or two to realise that she was looking at Xandros's chauffeur.

'Miss Gibbs?' he said politely, as if he'd never met her before. As if he hadn't witnessed Xandros kissing her so passionately on the back seat of the car. Or hadn't been forced to sit in a car outside her tiny house, waiting for his Greek boss to reappear over an hour later minus his tie, his hair dishevelled, his sensual mouth curved with pleasure.

Rebecca's cheeks burned with shame at the memory of that particular time. 'Where's Xandros?' she questioned, and then her eyes widened as a thousand horrible possibilities flooded into her mind. 'He's okay? I mean—nothing's happened to him?'

But the chauffeur's face might have been made of wood. Hard, disapproving wood—as if he was used to dealing with a hundred worried-looking women like Rebecca. 'Mr Alexandros Pavlidis asked me to convey his apologies, but he is dealing with a conference call. He asked me to bring you to him instead.'

Rebecca swallowed. *Bring you to him.* Like a convenience, she thought. A package. Something handy, but ultimately disposable. Yes, that was her, all right.

There was a split second while she ran through her options. What was the normal response when your lover sent his chauffeur to collect you and you suspected that was because your novelty value was wearing off and he might be tiring of you? Did you smile gratefully and thank the chauffeur and settle back comfortably in the back of the luxury car, counting your blessings?

Or would you be more respected—and desired—if you politely told the driver that he could go back to his boss with the information that you had changed your mind about dinner, and were staying in? That if he was busy, then surely the best solution was to leave him in peace to get on with his work.

But the lure of Xandros was strong, and so was her fear that a dramatic display of pique might bring about the end sooner than she had anticipated. Sooner than she could cope with.

'I'll get my coat,' she said.

The traffic was heavy and the weather bleak for a Thursday night in April. Rebecca's hair was whipped around her head by a biting wind as the hotel doorman opened the car door and she stepped out.

Had she been hoping that Xandros might have been standing in the foyer, waiting for her? That she wouldn't have to make the endless journey across the luxurious carpet on her own, imagining that eyes were on her, wondering who the woman in the cheap dress was? Wasn't there a part of her which was slightly ter-rified of being stopped by one of the hotel staff, demanding to know why she was taking the lift up to the penthouse?

But the journey passed without comment and in the mirror-lined lift she had the opportunity to drag a brush through her hair, to compose herself into the right kind of expression.

How did she look the first time he'd seen her—when he had hunted her down like a hungry predator? Surely she could recreate a similar kind of expression now. The kind of air which implied that she had a full and fulfilling life, and she wasn't particularly fussed about any man—not even if he *was* a world-famous Greek billionaire.

The trouble was that things changed. People changed, once a man like Xandros had possessed them. Did he have the power to turn women into his willing slaves—so that he could ultimately despise them for wanting him so badly?

Did he despise her? Had she no pride left where he was concerned?

The lift doors slid open noiselessly and she could hear the sound of his voice coming from the direction of the sitting room. A unique voice, in Rebecca's experience—low, soft, dangerous, sexy. He was speaking in Greek and then suddenly he switched to English as she began to walk towards its silken resonance, the heels of her boots quiet on the thick carpet.

He was sitting at the vast desk which overlooked London's Hyde Park, wearing a white silk shirt which contrasted against his deep olive skin. His ebony hair was ruffled and it sparkled with the light from drops of water—as if someone had scattered fine diamonds over his head, though he was clearly just out of the shower.

'Tell them no,' he was saying. 'Tell them…' And then he must have become aware of her presence for his gaze flicked up from the document he was reading. He studied her for one long, unhurried moment and then the black eyes glittered, and he gave a slow smile, running the tip of his tongue over his lips—like someone starving who had just seen their meal arrive.

'Tell them that they will have to wait,' he said softly, and then put the phone down without any kind of conventional goodbye. 'Rebecca,' he murmured. 'Rebecca *mou.*'

Usually, that deep, sensuous endearment made her tremble, but not tonight. 'Hello, Xandros,' she said evenly.

His eyes narrowed. Leaning back in his chair, he continued to study her. 'Forgive me for not coming to collect you myself—but some business came in which I had to deal with.'

Rebecca eyed the dark arrow of hair revealed by the few shirt buttons which had been left open and she felt the habitual rush of desire which overrode everything else, even sanity. But if she ignored this lapse in plain courtesy, then wasn't she just giving him permission to treat her any way he saw fit? If it was any other man, would she have said something? Of course she would. *But with any other man you wouldn't care!*

'You could have phoned.'

There was a split second of a pause. 'I could indeed,' he agreed steadily and felt the flicker of a pulse at his temple. *Be careful,* agape mou, he thought. *Be very careful.*

'And you're still not ready.'

His eyes narrowed. Was that a *criticism*? Of *him*? Did she not realise that he would not tolerate being judged? That no woman ever had, and no woman ever would? And was she not aware that she was in danger of treading the path of the predictable—the path that so many women before her had taken—and that if she did there could be only one outcome?

Leaning back in his chair just a little, he crossed one long leg over the other, watching the way that her eyes followed the movement as she tried to disguise the hunger in her eyes. Should he take her now? he wondered idly. Could he really be bothered to endure a restaurant dinner of small talk when all he wanted was to lose himself in the sweetness of her body?

'Indeed I am not,' he agreed softly, following her gaze to his bare feet and remembering that amazing time when she had… 'But that is easily remedied,' he said thickly. 'I shall go into the bedroom and finish getting dressed right now.'

'Okay,' she said uncertainly, something telling her that he was playing a game with her.

'Or…' His mouth flickered in the mockery of a smile. 'Or you could always come over here and say hello to me properly.'

Was that a subtle dig that she hadn't already done so? Rebecca was aware of some unknown emotion hovering in the air about them—something unspoken and dangerous. Instinct told her that she was playing with fire if she continued to moan about his lateness.

And an even stronger instinct made her badly want to kiss him.

Letting her handbag slide to the floor, she crossed the room and went over to him, bending her face to brush a light kiss against his lips. A kiss could wipe everything away, she thought longingly, her hands reaching up to his shoulders. *Oh, Xandros.*

'Nice,' he murmured. '*Oreos.* Do it some more.'

She kissed him again. And then again—only deeper this time and more intently—until he groaned and reached for her so that she let him pull her down onto his lap. 'Xandros!' she gasped.

'Touch me,' he urged, his mouth against her ear, his nostrils inhaling her light, flowery scent and feeling the silken spill of her hair next to his skin.

'Wh-where?'

'Where ever you want, *agape mou.*'

Oh, the choice was dazzling. Where did she begin? With his face—and all its shadowy contours, its contrasting lines and curves? She let her fingers caress his cheeks, running them along the luminously gold skin as if she were measuring the high angles of his cheekbones until she encountered the rasp of the dark new growth around his jaw.

'You didn't shave today,' she whispered.

'Yes, I did.'

'Oh.'

'Don't you know what they say about men who need to shave a lot?'

'No. What do they say?'

'What do you think they say?' he taunted. 'They say that he is a real man. Shall I prove it to you?' Taking her hand, he guided it down to between his legs and Rebecca felt the rush of blood to her cheeks as she felt the unbelievable hardness of him stretching the fabric of his elegant trousers. '*Ne*,' he groaned. 'Touch me there. Right there.'

'Like that?' she whispered, cupping him in the palm of her hand.

'*Ne*. More. Do that some more.'

She drifted her fingers teasingly over the rocky shaft of him, and his soft moan became an impatient imprecation. His ebony eyes were sparking pure passion and fire and his voice was unsteady as he stroked the silken skin above her breasts. 'I haven't seen this dress before.'

'Do you like it?'

'No. I want to tear it from your body.'

'Don't do that, Xandros—it's new.'

'Then why don't you take it off for me?'

Suddenly she felt shy, the doubts which had been assailing her all day coming back like spectres to haunt her. Was this an acceptable way to be treated by a man—to be made to feel insecure with him and then for him to ask you to perform a striptease, while he was still seated at his desk?

'Shouldn't we go into the bedroom?'

He gave a short laugh, but he was so hard and so hot for her that he doubted he would be able to make it to the door and this sensual power which she always seemed to exert over him made him want to wrest back control. 'Isn't it a little soon in our acquaintance for convention to rear its ugly head?'

Rebecca froze. *Acquaintance.* What kind of a word was *that*?

He saw her mouth tremble and he licked the tip of his tongue over it to cease its shiver, his hands slipping around her waist, fingers splaying over its slim indentation. 'Take it off,' he urged thickly.

She wanted to say *I can't*, but then he might ask her why, and how could she possibly answer that? Telling him that she wanted him to respect her and not just treat her as a sex object might sound like emotional blackmail. Respect had to be earned, not demanded—and, besides, maybe this was the kind of high-octane way in which billionaires conducted their love affairs.

And wasn't there a part of her which was revelling in her newly discovered ability to thrill him, to make his body rigid with tension, the black eyes opaque with a kind of helpless desire? Wasn't this the only time she felt that she had any real say in the relationship—in that emotionally and physically fraught time just before a couple had sex?

She stood up and lifted her hands to her hair, scooping it up between her fingers, before letting the whole heavy mass fall around her shoulders, watching his black eyes following the movement almost hypnotically. She knew he loved her hair. He had told her that the first time she'd met him—he'd said it was the colour of the setting sun before the night sky swallowed it up, whole. And when he had said it, he had looked as if he would like to swallow *her* up whole.

Hadn't it been his almost poetic way with words which had disarmed her just as much as the dark, good looks and the hard, lean body? The idea that a man could be the embodiment of all that was masculine and yet be unafraid to express himself in the way which would make a woman melt?

But hadn't that just been part of his well-practised seduction technique? How long had it been since he'd told her that her eyes were like the violet-blue flowers which scrambled in among the arid rocks and bloomed during a Grecian spring? Or that her skin was pure cream, and that was why he liked to lick it?

She shivered. Pride told her she should not strip for him and yet she knew that the evening would start off badly if she started playing games by refusing.

Peeling off her dress with one slow, sweeping movement, she dropped it on the desk, right in the middle of all his papers, daring him to object—*wanting* him to object. To somehow make this powerful man feel as helpless as she did. 'I do hope that won't interfere with your work,' she said, thinking no such thing at all.

'Rebecca,' he said unevenly.

'Yes, Xandros?'

'Turn around,' he said huskily. 'Turn around and let me feast my eyes on you.'

She made him wait. The only time she could—and then she began to walk to the other side of the desk.

'Rebecca?'

'Do you mean like this, Xandros? Do you want to see my bottom?' Slowly, she turned around and gave a flamboyant little wiggle and heard him laugh, but the laugh was tinged with a small groan as he saw the un-believably alluring scarlet briefs and the matching bra over which her breasts spilled.

'*Ne*. Just like that.'

He loved her bottom, as well as her hair. He had told her that, too, insisting that the pert globes be covered in nothing but lace, wanting to buy her sets of lingerie from one of the most exclusive stores in London—but she had refused. She would not be bought, even though sometimes he made her feel like a possession—just like one of his sleek cars or the fancy apartments he owned.

She began to slide the panties off, but her hands were trembling as she hooked them off over each foot and as she turned around, she crumpled them angrily between her palm and threw them at him.

Catching them effortlessly, Xandros raised his dark brows, and then—very deliberately—he lifted them up to his face and closed his eyes as he breathed in their scent.

Rebecca felt faint. What did he *do* to her? What power could he wield that could make her feel so utterly abandoned and wanton when she was with him—and yet leave her feeling abandoned in quite a different sense when he wasn't there?

'Delicious,' he murmured. 'Now the bra. Take it off.'

'You take it off.'

'But I can't reach.'

'Then move.'

'Are you ordering me around, *agape mou*?'

'You bet I am.'

Laughing softly, he rose to his feet and walked towards her with the slow stealth of the certain predator. And then, without warning, he snaked his arms around her and crushed her into his arms into a kiss of such hard—almost brutal—passion that she lost her balance.

But Xandros had her held firmly in his arms and he continued to kiss her, luxuriating in the softness of her body, enjoying the little cries she was making. For a woman who had made him wait longer than any other—his victory was almost complete.

'Still want to go to the bedroom?' he taunted, dragging his mouth away from hers. 'Or did you have somewhere else in mind?'

She no longer cared, but she was damned if she was going to tell him that. Or to give into him yet again. He wanted her now and he wanted her here and he could damned well wait as he had made her wait for him to turn up tonight.

'B-bed,' she managed. Damn him, damn him, damn him! Everything with him was a battle—but this was one she was going to win. She didn't *care* if it was conventional to want to go to the bedroom—at least it wouldn't be insultingly convenient to have him take her there and then on the floor as he had done so many times before.

But he scooped her up in his arms as she had known he would—and all her angry thoughts melted because this bit was *her* fantasy come true. Her darkly virile lover taking his willing captive off to experience the perfect pleasures of his body. Wasn't that the stuff of every woman's secret dream—to be mastered and dominated by such a powerful man?

Rebecca kissed his neck as he carried her down the long corridor of the suite he rented whenever he was in London—which took over the entire top floor of the

Park Lane hotel. She remembered the first time she had seen the bedroom—and had been rendered speechless.

Photo-spreads in glossy magazines could easily show luxury—but she'd been unaware that a single room could be so spacious. This one had a bed which was only slightly smaller than her entire bedroom back home—and everything else seemed to be controlled at the push of a button.

There was a giant TV screen and a small fridge, stocked with champagne and fancy chocolates as well as cut-glass bowls of flowers strategically placed to scent the room. There was even a bookcase and a rack which held all the international newspapers. But there was only one thing which she and Xandros did once they crossed the threshold of this room...

Xandros put her down on the bed and began to unbuckle his belt, watching her face as he did so, seeing her eyes darken in anticipation, as they always did. 'You want me to strip for you now?' he questioned softly.

'Yes. I-I insist on it,' she said unsteadily, but for her it was less of an erotic turn-on than the fact that she wanted to see *him* vulnerable—or as vulnerable as he was capable of.

But there was nothing remotely vulnerable about watching Xandros take his clothes off. First, he loosened his shirt, button by button—an interminable amount of buttons, or so it seemed to her.

'Want me to go faster?' he mocked as he saw her tongue snake out to moisten her parched lips.

Rebecca shook her head as he slipped the garment

from his broad, bare shoulders and let it flutter to the floor like the white flag of surrender—except she knew that he didn't have a surrendering bone in his body.

Rebecca saw him give a mocking wince as he slowly slid the zip of his trousers down and it said much for his self-possession and steely control that still he did not hurry it, despite the very obvious evidence of his arousal.

How could he possibly look both elegant and sexy as he removed his trousers and draped them over the back of a chair? His feet were bare, so all that remained were the silk boxer shorts which gave his body the look of a taut and supremely fit athlete. He kicked them off and for a moment just stood before her—completely naked and thrillingly aroused—his eyes glittering with an irresistible and arrogant challenge. And in that moment there was something so daunting—almost *forbiddingly* masculine—about him that Rebecca's heart thumped with something which felt more like fear than desire.

'Shall I come to you now, *agape mou*?' His voice was a caressing tease. 'Is that what you want?'

She wanted to tell him to promise not to break her heart, and she wanted him more than she could remember wanting anything in her life—more than breath itself. Was he aware of that? Or that sometimes he made her feel emotionally raw—as if he had seared away the top layer of her skin, leaving her cruelly exposed to his analytical eye? And what did that eye see? Someone who lived the way that plenty of other young women did—yet one who was dating a man way out of her league.

'If you want,' she answered, as if she couldn't care less.

He gave a low laugh of delight as he climbed onto the bed beside her. 'Come here.'

'No.'

'Ah, Rebecca. Rebecca *mou*.' Reaching out, he pulled her trembling body into the hard heat of his own, his thumb reflectively circling one puckered rose nipple so that it seemed to push insistently against him. 'You are still angry with me for being late?'

Tell him. *Tell* him! 'You could have let me know. I just don't want to be taken for granted, Xandros. I thought that you—'

His kiss silenced her, but then it was the most effective silencer in the world where women were concerned—and if all she was intending to do was to subject him to the age-old complaint about how a woman wanted to be treated, well… He had heard that grievance more times than he cared to remember.

This was better. Just this. The feel of skin against skin, the growing warmth of their ardour making their bodies closer still—as if they were glued together. In his arms, she was everything he could want from a lover—a little inexperienced, it was true, but he liked that. He had no time for women with lots of different party tricks to try out—for they were little better than hookers. A sense of wonder was fine by him, and, for however long the affair lasted, he would enjoy teaching her everything he knew.

He enjoyed the mental battle he engaged in during sex. He liked to test himself—to bring the woman to the near-height of pleasure over and over again, while denying himself until he could deny it no longer.

'Oh, Xandros,' she pleaded, with a frantic little cry of pleasure.

'Mmm?'

'Please!'

'Please, what, *agape mou*?'

'Now!'

How eager she was! How quickly she reached her peak! He lifted his dark head from where he had been suckling at her breast and moved over her, his black eyes glittering, before thrusting into her long and hard and deep, with a little groan of pleasure.

Sometimes he liked to watch a woman bloom and flower, but Rebecca was reaching her hands up to his shoulders, pulling him down so that their mouths met, and she groaned with pleasure as she writhed beneath him.

Tangled and gasping, she wrapped her limbs around him like a soft, white octopus, moving her hips in abandon until he felt the control slipping away from him. His orgasm came with a strength and a power which surprised him, but it had been like that with her since the very first time, and he couldn't quite work out why.

Because she had made him think the unthinkable— that he was actually going to fail to get her into his bed?

Her head lay against the stilling thunder of his heart and he stroked her hair, missing the absence of her warm breath as she turned her head away to stare at the wall, saying nothing.

Ironically, this was when he liked her best—when

she was retreating from him, like the tide moving away from the ever-distant shore. Xandros only wanted something when it was beyond his reach. Because once he had possessed it he wanted to move on, as he had been moving on all his restless life.

'Do you still want to go out for dinner?' He stretched lazily, and yawned. 'Or shall we stay here and order something in?'

For a moment, Rebecca didn't answer. In a way, she was perfectly happy to stay there—for she was as warm and replete as a woman could be. He would order from room service and the food would be wheeled in on a grand linen-covered trolley, with big silver domes concealing the food. And a silent waiter would set their table for them, while they watched him, rather awkwardly.

There would be flowers and fine wines and morsels of food which they would pick at—and, soon enough, they would return to bed. Or make love on the sofa, while watching a film. And Xandros would probably take at least one business call.

The alternative was to get dressed and be whisked off to dinner—and every woman liked a little life outside the private world of the bedroom, no matter how wonderful the fantasy land within it. If theirs was a normal relationship she would have been thrilled to have been seen with him—but it wasn't. They weren't supposed to be dating and so they crept around, like thieves in the night. They visited discreet, out-of-the-way restaurants—or they stayed in his hotel room. Sometimes she wondered if anyone would actually believe her if she told them she was seeing the Greek billionaire.

But who could she tell? She had put her job on the line by agreeing to date him in the first place and none of her colleagues knew about it.

She turned her head to look at him, touching the strong curve of his jaw with the tip of her finger, and her heart turned over. Was she being selfish by wanting to go out? He looked so tired. Suddenly, her doubts and her fears melted away and she snuggled closer against his warm body, wrapping her arms around his broad shoulders and massaging the silken skin beneath. Was it inbuilt in a woman that she should want to nurture her man?

'Which would *you* prefer?' she questioned softly. 'To stay here?'

Xandros bit back an instinctive click of impatience. He wanted to tell her not to keep accommodating *his* needs. But this was inevitably what happened. Women tried to please you and in so doing they submerged their own identity into yours. And then you lost sight of what had attracted you to them in the first place— for you could no longer see it.

'What I would prefer is to stay right here,' he said brutally. 'But I am afraid that if I do that, then I'll fall asleep and I've booked the Pentagram for nine—and you told me how much you'd always wanted to go there. So you had better make your mind up.'

'Then I guess we'd better go.' Could his curt response be any better reminder that this particular man didn't *need* any nurturing? She moved, her thigh brushing against his as she stretched—wondering if that would be enough to have him pull her back hungrily into his arms, but he didn't. She gave him a quick smile, but it was one which was edged with nerves. 'I'll go and get dressed.'

He lay back against the pillows and watched her move across the room. She was both graceful and beautiful, he thought—but he recognised that something was changing between them. Something as inevitable as the sun rising in the sky each morning. The predictable had reared its ugly head. Xandros couched his words with velvet in an attempt to lessen their blow. 'Because of course,' he said softly, 'this may well be the last chance we get to have dinner for some time.'

Her footsteps halted as Rebecca froze. Carefully composing herself, she slowly turned around, her heart beginning to beat hard beneath her breast as she considered the possible implication of his words—but she prayed that her face gave nothing away. 'What are you talking about?'

'Didn't I tell you?' he questioned carelessly. 'I have to fly back to New York tomorrow.'

Don't react, she told herself. *Stay calm.* 'Oh? For very long?'

He could see her face working to conceal her disappointment and he gave a shrug, for his timetable was his own. He would not have disclosed it even if he'd known it, because freedom was as important to Xandros as breathing. 'It is impossible to predict. A fortnight at least. Maybe longer—depending on the deal.'

'How absolutely lovely,' she said, with the bright enthusiasm of a travel agent. 'I expect the city is beautiful at this time of year.'

'Yes, it is,' he agreed. Yet in a perverse kind of way, Xandros was disappointed that she was accepting it so easily. Hadn't he been anticipating some kind of scene which might have heralded the end? If she had objected or sulked that would have been it. He would have finished it without a second thought, because no woman had the right to question his movements, no matter how much pleasure he brought them in bed or how much they had begun to paint rosy pictures of the possibility of a future together.

But she turned and began to walk out of the bedroom—presumably in search of the clothes she had so delectably removed—and he felt his body stir at the sight of the high, firm curve of her naked bottom. And suddenly Xandros knew that he still hadn't got her out of his system. His tongue snaked out over bone-dry lips and his words caught her on the threshold of the room. 'But I will see you when I return, *agape mou.*'

It was a statement, not a request. Rebecca felt like a mouse who had been played with by a large cat—and then had her fate spared at the very last moment. 'You might. If you're lucky,' she said, in a light, who-cares voice which she thought sounded pretty convincing.

Thank heavens he couldn't see her face—because surely he would have read her almost dizzy relief that he *was* coming back. And that he *was* planning to see her again. Or was he clever enough to guess at her dreadful, aching realisation that one day soon it would all be over and it was going to feel a million times worse than this?

Her hands were trembling by the time she reached the sitting room and began to pick up her clothes, wondering how the hell she had let this happen——to have got herself into something she'd known was hopeless from the very start. And wishing that she could have sustained the strength of character which had attracted him to her in the beginning. In the days when it had been so easy to refuse him.

CHAPTER TWO

THEIR paths should never have crossed, of course. Ordinary, suburban girls like Rebecca weren't supposed to rub shoulders with jet-setting billionaires like Alexandros Pavlidis.

But Rebecca worked as a flight attendant for a small and highly exclusive private airline which brought her into contact with the kind of people that most mere mortals only read about.

Evolo airline was based close to London and ferried its mega-rich customers around the world for astronomical fees. It paid Rebecca more than any of the bigger airlines would have done, but in return required her to be available at very little notice and, above all, to be discreet.

Rock stars, Hollywood actors, minor royals and just the plain rich frequented the champagne-fuelled flights which had been started by an ambitious blonde pilot named Vanessa Gilmour.

Each time she flew, Vanessa or her male deputy would brief Rebecca on the passenger list and one morning she had seen a name she didn't recognise. A rather beautiful name.

'Who's this?' she asked, tongue twisting over the words. 'Alexandros Pavlidis?'

Vanessa pulled a funny kind of face. 'Don't you ever read the newspapers?'

'Sometimes.' Rebecca pulled her uniform cap down over her smoothed-down hair and smiled. 'But I prefer books.'

'He's an architect,' explained Vanessa, an impatient wave of her hand dismissing the entire concept of books. 'Or *star*chitect as the press like to refer to him. A Greek based in New York—he's designing a new bank near London Bridge. I met him at a party and persuaded him that Evolo could accommodate his every need. It's the first time he's flown with us—and I don't want it to be the last. So be nice to him, Rebecca—just not *too* nice.'

Rebecca heard the warning in her employer's voice—although she didn't need one. She knew it was forbidden to date any of the customers. 'What's he like?' she checked politely, because as crew they were supposed to know about the passengers' likes and dislikes.

There was a pause. 'He's difficult,' admitted Vanessa softly. 'Very difficult.' And then her eyes sparkled in a way that Rebecca had never seen them do before as her voice dropped into a kind of ecstatic whisper. 'And absolutely bloody *gorgeous*.'

If difficult was an understatement, then so was gorgeous, Rebecca decided when she met him later that day. She found herself startled by the man's overwhelming charisma as well as his astonishing good looks.

If someone had said, 'Bring me the most delectable man in the world,' then Alexandros Pavlidis would have been the list-topper. If you wanted tall, dark, ruggedly handsome—with a coldly irresistible air about him—then Pavlidis ticked all the right boxes.

The Greek was terse to the point of rudeness, and he operated at the speed of light—the retinue who were following his tall, black-clad figure into the small departure lounge almost having to run to keep up with his long-legged stride.

And it didn't escape her notice that every woman who worked in the building found some kind of pretext to try to catch a glimpse of him.

But it wasn't her job to swoon over customers. Her manner had to remain benignly courteous and respectful. Whatever he asked for, she brought. She did not attempt to engage him in any kind of conversation and her entire dialogue with him was confined to politely answering his requests.

He began to use Evolo regularly for his European trips, since apparently he had sold his own private jet fleet for environmental reasons, and his work took him all over the globe. Rebecca tried not to be so heart-poundingly aware of him, but it wasn't easy. She couldn't quash the excitement she always experienced when she saw his name on the passenger list.

And even though she did her best to disguise it a kind of unspoken awareness began to sizzle between the two of them—because nothing could disguise chemistry, no matter how hard you tried. His black eyes would narrow thoughtfully when he saw her, and her heart would leap whenever he dealt her his rare, slow smile.

But she remembered Vanessa's words about discretion and boundaries and quickly turned away from it. Even if it wasn't forbidden to date the clients—was she really considering herself the kind of woman that someone like Xandros *would* date?

Yet her apparent lack of interest seemed to inflame him. He went out of his way to engage her in conversation and surely it would have been discourteous not to have joined in?

'What are you doing once we land?' he asked her one dark, starry night as the plane touched down in Madrid.

'I'm having an early night,' she answered.

'Ah!' His black eyes glittered with sudden understanding, for this would explain her inexplicable resolve not to flirt with him. He felt a slight pang of disappointment, but it was quickly followed by the inevitable rush of challenge—for there was no rival who could not be easily dispatched if Xandros wanted something. 'And who is the lucky man?'

Rebecca felt colour tinge her cheeks. 'Mr Pavlidis!'

'*Ne, agape mou,* what is it?'

Why did he *call* her that? Didn't it mean 'darling', or something? 'Will that be all?'

'*Ochi,*' he said roughly, for he had seen her blush—something which was as rare as the rose-coloured Starlings which sometimes appeared on the Aegean islands. 'It will not be all. I want you to have dinner with me. In fact, I demand it.'

Maybe if she had agreed to his request then it would have all been over before it began, but Rebecca did something that few women ever did. She said no.

When a man had everything—he wanted what he couldn't have, and Xandros wanted Rebecca. He wanted her in a way he hadn't wanted a woman for years and he was forced to pursue her—something which was almost alien to him. Even when he'd first arrived in New York as an unsophisticated eighteen-year-old, women had fallen eagerly into his arms.

'What harm is there in dinner?' he mused, the next time they flew together. It was a late winter afternoon as the luxury jet began its descent towards Paris and the early-setting sun was lighting the sky with its fiery blaze. Coal-black eyes mocked her. 'Do not worry.' His voice was like silk, embroidered with sardonic thread. 'You have turned me down enough times to impress me, *agape mou*. And now that we have established your fine reputation, you can see there is no reason for us not to enjoy one another's company.'

It sounded unbearably tempting. Rebecca tugged unnecessarily at the neat jacket of her Evolo uniform. 'But I'm not supposed to mix with the customers, Mr Pavlidis,' she said.

'Says who?'

'Says my boss.'

'This would be Vanessa?' he queried, his eyes narrowing.

'That's right.'

He nodded, as if satisfying himself of something. Or someone. 'Vanessa has her own agenda,' he drawled softly. 'And I'm not proposing that we ride off into the sunset together,' he added sarcastically. 'I just think Paris is not a city to be alone in and that it would be agreeable to have a little company. Mmm? What could be wrong with that?'

His black eyes glittered with enticing question. In her heart, Rebecca knew that he wasn't being straight-forward with her; she suspected he had an address book crammed with the numbers of beautiful and willing women no matter how many cities he visited. But she had held out for so long against her feelings for him and in that moment she felt defenceless against the full onslaught of his charm.

'Just dinner?' she verified breathlessly.

'If that is what you want,' Xandros returned, his smile careless.

It hadn't been 'just' dinner, of course. For how could you not let a man like Xandros kiss you at the end of it when you had been longing for him to kiss you since the first time you'd set eyes on him? And then? Her battle had been with herself rather than with him. Her sense of what was right and proper vying with her heart and her body's desires.

She had lost the battle. Of *course* she had ended up in bed with him. He was a powerful, virile man who would not be satisfied with a chaste kiss at the end of a first date—and for the first time in her life, neither was she.

Rebecca had never felt so physically vulnerable beneath a man's caresses as she was to Xandros. She hated herself for her easy capitulation that night and yet she couldn't stop herself. Her hungry body's need overrode everything else—ruthlessly quelling the voice in her head which demanded to know whether he would respect her after this.

And to Xandros, her only spoken objection was a practical one. 'No one from work must know,' she told him urgently as his hand began its inevitable and longed-for journey up her inner thigh.

'Why should they?' he breathed, peeling off her panties with a low moan of delight.

'Because…*oh…oh…Xandros*! Because people…' She closed her eyes, and swallowed. 'They talk,' she whispered eventually.

'Then we won't give them anything to talk about,' he assured her silkily, his fingers working ruthlessly against her hotly aroused flesh, feeling it yield to him. 'No one will know a thing. We will keep it secret, *ne*? Our little secret…'

But weren't secrets wrong? Wasn't that making it sound as if he wanted to keep her hidden away— like something furtive, to be ashamed of? Rebecca tried to pull away, but the lure of his embrace was too strong to resist, the gentle caress of his fingertips too tremblingly intense. 'Xandros?' she tried, one last time.

'*Ochi*,' he negated fiercely. 'Say nothing! Do nothing but stay here in my arms when you know that this is what we both want!' And he kissed her into willing submission.

Yet even at the height of her very first orgasm, Rebecca was aware of a sharp twist of pain in her heart. That her surrender could be her emotional undoing, and that she risked losing everything—the most important thing being her heart. Her life and her future was one in which a man like Xandros would have no place— and yet, having tasted all the pleasures that he gave her, the thought of any future without him already seemed bleak and empty.

If she had known all that right from the beginning, then why hadn't she stopped? Why give into something which you knew instinctively was doomed on so many levels?

Because human nature wasn't like that. It made you reach out and grab at the unreachable.

The mists of memory cleared as Rebecca blinked around at her luxurious surroundings. She bent down to pick up one of the shoes she had discarded while she had been stripping off for her hard-bodied Greek lover and sighed. It was pointless going back over what had happened. She could do nothing to change the past—what she *could* work on was the present.

But the present brought her scant comfort.

She was here, in Xandros's penthouse suite—about to go out for a meal which she knew that neither of them really wanted. And after that he was off to New York, and she didn't know when she was going to see him again. So how was she going to play it? Did she have enough acting ability to convince him that she didn't really care, either way—or would he see right through her?

'Rebecca?'

The silken, accented Greek voice filtered through the air. By concentrating on finishing fastening her shoes, Rebecca was able to compose herself before straightening up to look at him. His black eyes were set like dark jewels in the backdrop of his gleaming olive skin and her heart turned over with love and longing. If only he didn't look so heartbreakingly gorgeous. Reaching into her handbag, she took out a hairbrush and began to make great sweeping strokes through hair all tousled from love-making. 'Yes, Xandros?' she questioned calmly.

He liked to watch her brush her hair. The first time she had loosened it for him he had told her that it was the colour of Greek honey—which was darker and richer than any honey in the world. 'The car is waiting downstairs, *agape mou.*' His eyes narrowed at her in question. 'You still want to go and eat?'

What would he say if she told him the truth—that what she really wanted was to know how he felt about her? Whether he *was* tiring of her—or whether it was a figment of her over-active imagination. But some bone-deep instinct told her that a man like Xandros would ultimately despise a woman who wanted that kind of reassurance. To an independent man that might smack of neediness—and everyone knew how unattractive *that* was.

'Eat? I thought you'd never ask,' she said lightly, turning her head so that her newly brushed hair swung in a scented curtain around her still-flushed cheeks. She even managed to give him a faintly mocking look in return. 'Somehow I've worked up quite an appetite—though can't for the life of me work out why!'

Xandros gave a barely perceptible nod as he picked up her coat and held it open for her, watching the naturally sinuous movement of her body as she wriggled into it. Her response had held just the right amount of cool distance and yet her apparent composure was strong enough to fan the flames of his desire once more. He found himself wanting to pull her back into his arms again and a nerve flickered at his temple.

This was going to be harder to finish than he had anticipated.

CHAPTER THREE

NEXT morning Rebecca awoke to the sound of a shower splashing nearby and Xandros singing something rather tunelessly in Greek. He sounded happy, she thought wistfully—and why wouldn't he be? She opened her eyes and stared at the chandelier which glittered above the vast bed like a canopy of diamonds.

Over dinner last night, he had described the elegant new apartment block he was building, which incorporated a 'sky-garden' at its summit which would bring lush grasses and fragrant shrubs to the defiantly urban part of the city in which it was set. He wanted it to be the first of many—to bring greenery to grey places. He wanted a world which did not push nature out. His deep voice had been passionate and dreamy and Rebecca had found herself swept up by it—torn between admiration and envy. It had been as if he was describing a paradise she would never be part of.

She heard the gushing of the water stop and after a few minutes he walked into the bedroom—completely naked—towelling at his ebony hair with a small towel.

His hard body glowed, the broad shoulders tapering

down into narrow hips and then long, hair-roughened legs. He was a man utterly at ease with his nudity—but then who wouldn't be with a physique like that? He swam every day, no matter where he was in the world. He had told her that it was one thing he had brought with him from his native Greece—the desire to feel the water on his skin and the delicious freedom which came with it.

He looked at her lying amidst the rumpled sheets and his mouth softened briefly into a smile. *'Kherete,'* he said softly.

'Hello,' she murmured back, astonished at how she could still feel almost shy when he looked at her like that—despite the fact that he knew her body more thoroughly than any other man had ever done. 'I feel so lazy I can't move.'

'Seeing you lying there like that makes me want to stay.'

Easy to say. 'But you can't.'

'No.' He slid on a pair of dark boxers which felt silky next to his skin. 'Unfortunately I can't. As soon as I get off the plane, stateside, I have a long list of meetings to attend.' He looked up and shrugged but his black eyes gleamed with anticipation. 'There is a big deal nearing completion, new plans to draw up.'

'And no doubt a stack of invitations to glittering parties from just about every New York society hostess worth her salt.' She hadn't meant to say it, but somehow the words seemed to tumble out of their own accord.

There was the fraction of a pause, the faintest elevation of jet-dark brows. 'That, too,' he agreed.

Rebecca knew that she was stepping into unfamiliar territory. That Xandros, more than most men, compartmentalised his life—and she was firmly fixed in the English section. But surely showing interest wouldn't necessarily be interpreted as possessive jealousy? Didn't dating him give her the rights to know *something* about his life? 'And do you go to them?'

'To parties?' He shrugged as he reached into the closet for a pure silk shirt in a buttery ivory colour and, slipping it on over his broad shoulders, began to button it. 'Sometimes—like most people—when I'm not too busy. Why wouldn't I?' He pulled on a pair of dark trousers. 'And what about you, Rebecca—what do you do when your Greek lover is not in town?'

Was it significant that he was asking her this now—when he had never really been interested before? Or was he simply being dutiful and turning the question back on her? Pride made her want to embellish a life which would surely sound very ordinary when judged by his standards. Imagine how he would react if she told him that she spent a lot of her free time thinking about him! Even the supermarket was an unsafe zone, for she often found herself scouring the shelves for the brand of olive oil she knew that his family firm produced back in Greece. Up until now, she'd never found it.

'Oh, this and that.' She pushed a stray lock of hair out of her eyes. 'I go out to the cinema—sometimes the theatre—'

'With your girlfriends, of course?' he cut in, his fingers pausing in the act of zipping up his trousers.

Something in his dismissive tone offended her. Who

did he think he was? He offered her nothing, nor promised her anything—did he think she just crawled into a dark box and stayed there when he was out of the country, like some caged animal eagerly panting for his return?

'Not always. Obviously, I have friends of both sexes.'

Brilliant black eyes were fixed on her and he shot the word out as if it were a bullet. 'Men?'

There was a pause. Did he imagine these were the Dark Ages? 'Of course.'

'Men that you go out with?'

Rebecca sat up in bed, her hair now tumbling down all over her bare breasts. 'Not *go out* with!' she protested. She wanted to say, Not like I go out with you— but that would have sounded false. They didn't exactly *go out*, did they? They just got together for some very agreeable sex whenever he happened to be in town. That he bought her dinner or occasionally took her to a show was neither here nor there. 'Just men whose company I occasionally enjoy. You know.'

His eyes narrowed, fiercely intelligent, hard and, in that one moment, displaying a flash of something which looked almost like cruelty.

'No, I don't know. You are not making any sense to me, *agape mou*. In my experience men and women who go out together have only one real item on their agenda. For that is how nature intended it.'

His silky voice sounded almost…*threatening*. And *primitive*. Rebecca frowned, taken aback by the hot storm of accusation which blazed from his eyes. 'What are you suggesting, Xandros?' she queried unsteadily.

'That I have sex with other men while you aren't here?'

'Do you?'

First she felt faint, then hurt—and then angry. But it was difficult to maintain your dignity while you were completely naked and Rebecca yanked the sheet from the bed and wrapped it around herself. As she got out of bed she realised that her hands were shaking and she turned on him.

'I can't believe you would even *ask* a question like that! Implying I'm some kind of…some kind of…*tramp*!' Her breath was coming hot and rapid and he regarded her with a narrow-eyed scrutiny before crossing the room, but she waved him away. 'Just what kind of woman do you normally associate with to make you think something like that?' she demanded.

None that had as much fire in their eyes as she did at that precise moment, he thought with a mixture of sexual hunger and something much darker which had not reared its ugly head for a long time. With an effort he forced himself back from its brink. For a man who rarely considered himself to be in the wrong, apology did not come easy. 'It was a clumsy question—I should never have asked it.'

'No, you shouldn't.'

He reached out for her and he could see the struggle taking place within her, telling herself not to forgive him too quickly. Until, with a reluctant sigh, she let him lift her hand to his lips and he managed to coax a reluctant softening of her mouth as he kissed each fingertip in turn.

'Forgive me,' he murmured, against skin which still

carried his scent from their long night of sex. 'Forgive me, *agape mou.*'

She wanted to—and yet she wanted to tell him to go to hell. Wavering between desire and despair, Rebecca closed her eyes, wishing she were strong enough to walk away from this sweet torture he inflicted on her. And when she opened them again it was to find his gaze upon her—dark and unremitting and gleaming with erotic promise. When he looked at her that way, she was utterly lost—so did that make her weak, or him strong? Or both? *Oh, Xandros.*

'Do you?' he prompted her.

With an effort, she shrugged, thankful he didn't have the power to read her thoughts. She might not want to let him go, but she was damned if she was going to lie down on the ground and let him trample all over her. 'I'll think about it.' Her eyes grew serious. 'But please don't ever accuse me of something like that again. It's unjustified and it's archaic.'

Was it? 'But I am Greek,' he returned softly. 'And we Greeks understand that human nature never really changes. I believe that it is impossible for a man and a woman to have real friendship—for how can they, when the hungry presence of sex is for ever in the background? Particularly when the woman happens to look like you, Rebecca.' His mouth twisted into an odd kind of smile as he forced himself to voice the inevitable climb-down. 'But I accept that you have no intention of bedding another man.' And why would she, when Xandros Pavlidis was the finest lover a woman could ever desire in a hundred lifetimes?

He could see her looking as if she wanted something more—and this wearied him because he did not provide emotional security. Ever. Xandros used exactly the same coolly analytical attitude towards relationships as he did towards his work. Affairs ran their course—in the same way as a fever did—and by now he had gone through most of the stages with Rebecca.

He had chased her and seduced her. Revelled in making love to her—over and over and over again. But much more and the relationship would slip into a boring and predictable pattern—and Xandros would not tolerate either. Much better for it to finish on a high. To leave him with exquisite memories, rather than the slow deterioration into apathy.

Yet even though he sensed that his time with her was coming to an end, something inside him relented. A little longer, that was all he wanted. Because somehow—unusually—he had not quite got her out of his system and he needed more time to rid his mind and his body of her sweet temptations. He felt the sweet, hard jerk of desire.

'I should be back on the tenth,' he murmured. 'So why don't you plan something around that? Something you'd really like—a place you've always wanted to visit. Bill it to me.'

Rebecca flinched as one of his phones began to ring, but he didn't even appear to notice the wounding nature of his words—dropping a brief kiss on the tip of her nose, his mind already occupied with the day ahead.

'I'll call you,' he promised as he clicked one of the buttons to answer it. *Soon,* he mouthed, beginning to speak rapidly in Greek as she headed for one of the bathrooms.

Rebecca felt distracted all the way home. And hurt—the kind of simmering low-grade hurt which wouldn't go away. Usually, when Xandros flew out she treated herself to chocolates or bubble bath, or a new book—silly little inexpensive treats which helped lessen the impact of his departure. But today she didn't feel like buying any. Nor did she feel like an early night, which was the sensible solution after so little sleep— with a flight the next day leaving soon after dawn.

Plan something, he had said.

Bill it to me, he had said. Was he aware of how dismissive those words had been—as if everything in life came with a price-tag? She supposed that maybe for Xandros it did. Did he think that she couldn't manage to provide an enjoyable time on her rather limited income? It was true that her salary as a stewardess was a mere drop in the ocean compared to his vast wealth—but she knew how to live. You didn't need vintage wines and costly foods to satisfy your appetite.

Rebecca shut the front door behind her and looked around. Yet she hadn't exactly welcomed him into *her* home, had she? Why, Xandros had barely been here apart from a few bouts of snatched passion *en route* to somewhere else. He had certainly never eaten a meal here or spent the night with her in her—admittedly— rather small bed. But it *wasn't* small—it was a normal, double bed. It was just that anything was going to seem minute when compared with what he was used to.

Putting the kettle on to make a cup of coffee, she stared out of the window where the first hint of green buds were softening the sharp edges of the branches. Springtime often brought with it clarity—shining a light after the long darkness of winter—and maybe it was time for her to face facts.

She was falling ever deeper for Xandros, but currently their relationship was all on his terms. She was worried about it ending and yet how could anything so one-sided possibly be sustained?

Surely Xandros got fed-up with everyone always acceding to *his* whims. An appetite would inevitably become jaded if it was always indulged. Didn't you need a proper contrast in life to enjoy it to the max?

Plan something, he had said.

Rebecca's mouth curved into a sudden, spontaneous smile. She most certainly would! Only she wouldn't dream of billing it to him. He would get a taster of life, Rebecca-style! A little home-cooking and a flavour of the ordinary.

She decided to make him a home-made chicken pie—a favourite choice from her childhood and something he'd be unlikely ever to get in one of the fancy restaurants he frequented. Going down the road to her local wine merchant, she bought a mid-price bottle of red which the wine-merchant said was a real find. Next, she set to giving her apartment the kind of spring-cleaning which it hadn't seen in longer than she cared to remember.

How satisfying it was to drag out pieces of furniture and to polish and wipe and shine in all the dusty corners. It was liberating—and Rebecca felt as if she were cleaning out all the dark corners of her own mind as she scrubbed and polished.

Xandros hadn't rung, but she wasn't going to get into a flap about it. She wasn't going to be needy and dependent when he was obviously busy. He had said the tenth, and that was what she was planning for.

She washed the linen on the bed—hanging it out on her tiny washing line in between April showers so that it smelt all clean and fresh. But as she ironed it and sniffed it with the enthusiasm of someone appearing in a soap-powder commercial she felt a faint cloud of apprehension skitter into her mind. Just because she was planning to entertain Xandros on *her* territory, didn't mean she had to transform herself into some kind of hausfrau, did it?

And besides, Xandros still hadn't phoned—and once she registered the long gap since they'd spoken she began to fret about it, even though she tried to tell herself not to.

She did that dreadful thing of haunting the telephone—while gazing in dismay at the vases of fresh flowers she'd bought down at the market. What if they'd wilted by the time he turned up? What if all the dust particles she'd cleared away somehow regrouped on every lovingly buffed piece of furniture?

It was that thought which drew her up short and made her realise that, although she was planning to give Xandros a little taste of *her* life, she was still behaving like a starving dog who was content to be thrown an occasional scrap from its master's table.

Why was she waiting for him to call her? She knew his number. She shared his bed—why shouldn't she call *him* to confirm the arrangements?

Yet despite all the reasoning in the world her hands

were still trembling as she dialled his number and her heart was pounding with nerves. How stupid was *that*? This was a person with whom she had…

There was a sudden click on the line and then an automated voice telling her that her call was being transferred, then more ringing—with the instruction to leave a message. She had nothing prepared. Nothing to say but a stumbled, 'Oh, hello, Xandros, it's me. Rebecca. I was just…'

Just what? Just wondering what time to put the chicken pie in the oven? *Very* enticing.

'I was just calling to say hi,' she continued firmly. 'And perhaps you could give me a ring when you're free?' Now she sounded like a dental receptionist asking him to confirm that he was about to keep his appointment.

Then she noticed that there was another number listed for him, and when she tried that, a woman's voice answered.

Rebecca's heart pounded painfully in her chest. *Who the hell are you?* 'Is…is Xandros there, please?'

'Not at the moment, I'm afraid,' came the woman's cool, transatlantic drawl. 'May I ask who's calling?'

I'm his *girlfriend*, she wanted to shout. 'Could you just tell him that Rebecca called?'

'Sure.'

Her phone shrilled into life an hour later and a distracted-sounding Xandros spoke. 'You rang?'

She wanted to ask who the woman had been. She wanted to ask why he never rang when he said he would. Instead, she said in a way which would afterwards make her cringe, 'Did I disturb you?'

There was a pause. 'I was in a meeting.' One of those meetings with a developer who seemed to think that cutting corners was a necessary part of construction. It had gone on for much too long, and it still wasn't resolved. 'What can I do for you, Rebecca?'

Was she imagining the indifference in his voice? Was this why she had always waited for *him* to ring before? Some instinct protecting her from this haughty coolness which seemed curiously at odds with the hot passion he displayed in bed. He was a man who always liked to be in control by telephoning her; she was taking a little of the control back.

But the reason she was doing this was because she wanted things to move out of the rut they seemed stuck in. To become once more the sparky and animated woman she used to be. 'I just wanted to check that you're still arriving on Friday.'

Narrowing his eyes, Xandros glanced down at the diary lying open on his desk. 'That's right. Though if this deal isn't tied up, I may have to take a later flight.' His voice softened by a fraction as he allowed himself an enticing reminder of just how beautifully she always welcomed him. 'Why don't I call you when I land and you can come straight round and say hello, *agape*? Tell you what, why don't I warn the hotel—and you can be right there waiting for me?'

Warn the hotel? The husky timbre of his voice left her in no doubt as to how he would like her to greet him. Probably wearing a tight, satin bra and a pair of skimpy panties. She thought of the chicken pie she had laboured over. The apartment which was so clean, it looked as if she were about to start marketing it. And the little vase of lily of the valley which she had rather self-consciously placed next to her bed, which she planned to make up with clean and freshly ironed linen.

'I'd much rather you came to me actually, Xandros.'

There was another pause. 'To you?'

'Yes. I'm cooking you dinner here. At my apartment. Just for a change.'

In New York, Xandros frowned and stifled a sigh. He didn't *want* her cooking for him. He wanted her where he always had her—on tap and readily available. Quietly, he began to drum two fingers against the gleaming oak of his desk. 'What is the point of wasting precious time cooking when there are so many more enjoyable ways of spending it?' he questioned reasonably.

But Rebecca was determined—she could feel her resolve bubbling to the surface. She was no longer going to be just a compliant sex-object—available whenever and wherever. From now on they were going to be on a more equal footing—because that was how relationships moved forward.

'Because I want to,' she said stubbornly.

Oh, do you? 'Then who am I to object?' questioned Xandros, with silky carelessness. 'In that case—I'll come straight from the airport, and ring you when I'm on my way. How does that sound—satisfied now?'

But Rebecca was not left with anything remotely resembling satisfaction as he finished the call with a note in his voice she couldn't ever remember hearing before. Instead, a terrible kind of foreboding had begun to make her stomach flutter and she felt as if she had stupidly brought down the curtain on the show, before the last act was properly over.

CHAPTER FOUR

XANDROS had been to Rebecca's house before—but maybe he'd never looked at it properly. When a man was hot with desire it obliterated almost everything else and he had wanted her so badly. She had made him wait for so long that the sex had been dynamite. He hadn't been able to get enough of her.

And now? His thumb jammed on the doorbell. Of course he still wanted her, but inevitably desire became corrupted. Life and circumstances began to muddy it. More damningly, women always had to try and change what was good—and to reach beyond that. Why did they always want more than you were prepared to give and thus to ruin it for themselves? Xandros felt his mouth thin into a grim line. They hid their duplicity and schemes behind their beautiful smiles and men allowed them to. Why, he would never forget the shock on his father's face when his mother had announced she was leaving them. How could a man be such a fool not to have seen it coming? How could he and Kyros not have seen it coming?

Her front door flew open. Hair piled up on top of

her head and an apron tied around the waist of her short cotton dress—this was Rebecca looking more functional than he had ever seen her. Her smile was bright, but he thought he could detect a wariness in her eyes. Had she recognised that she had pushed him into a corner and realised her folly too late?

But Xandros had played out this scene often enough in the past that he'd become a master of it and knew how best to deal with it. He had his props to hand, just as she had hers. He could hear the sound of music playing and smell something cooking.

'Hello, Rebecca,' he said softly.

'Hello, Xandros.' She stood there, almost awkwardly, not quite knowing what to do, or say. A fish out of water in her own home. 'Won't you come in?'

He gave an odd kind of smile as he walked into the tiny hallway and shut the door behind him. How he hated convention—the stultifying feeling that this kind of situation imposed on him. Trying to ignore the line of shoes which were lined up by the telephone—how cluttered!—he stared down into her violet-blue eyes. 'No kiss?' he mused.

She wound her arms up around his neck, her inexplicable nerves and his heady proximity making her tremble—but once his lips crushed down on hers, then all her vague fears were forgotten. How could they be otherwise? The seeking caress of his kiss and the hard contours of his body stirred her into instant longing as she gave herself up to his kiss and with a hungry groan he deepened it.

His hands began to rove experimentally over her body and once again he was taken aback by the intensity of his desire—his body felt like dry timber, her kiss the match which ignited it. He wanted her here, now—instantly. If he could have signed a pact at that moment to say that he wanted to spend the rest of his life inside her body, then he would have signed it willingly. 'Oh, Rebecca,' he groaned. 'What is it that you do to me?'

'X-Xandros,' she breathed, because he was splaying his fingers luxuriously over her bottom and bringing her up against the hard cradle of his own desire.

'*Ne, agape mou?* What is it that you want? Some of this? Ah, yes—you like that, don't you? And this? Mmm? This, too?'

His fingers were teasing their way over her belly and he was drifting his mouth against her neck in a way which was making her shiver even more. She knew what he wanted—exactly the same as her—but tonight was going to be different. Tonight she wanted to feel more than just an object in his arms.

She pulled away from him, her cheeks flushed, her heart beating like crazy. 'There'll be time for that later—but I don't want your supper ruined.'

How like a suburban housewife she sounded! But Xandros didn't react. Didn't she realise what she sounded like? Didn't she realize how many times women had spoiled things for themselves through their own, warped ambition? 'No, indeed—for that would indeed be a crime,' he said gravely. 'To ruin my supper.'

Rebecca smiled uneasily. 'Come on through.'

Xandros walked into the sitting room, which had a dining area at one end, and a door leading into the tiny kitchen. It was smaller than his walk-in closet back in New York and once he had made love to her on that rather curious sofa while his chauffeur waited outside. But tonight the scene was very different and she had clearly gone to a lot of trouble.

Candles glittered everywhere and there was a small pot of flowers placed at the centre of the table, which was laid for dinner—every piece of cutlery and china seeming to be fighting for a little of the limited space. The smell of polish clashed with the heavy smell of something cooking, and Xandros forced a smile.

'It smells delicious,' he lied.

'Does it? I hope you're hungry.'

He guessed that now would not be a good time to tell her that he had eaten something on the plane. 'Why don't we have a drink first?'

'Yes, of course—sorry, I should have asked. Would wine be all right?'

'Some wine would be perfect,' he said evenly, and took the bottle from her and began to open it. 'Here, let me.'

The glasses were chinking like wind chimes as she put them down in front of them. Would he notice that was because her hands were shaking—and how stupid was *that*? Xandros was her lover and she was entertaining him for the first time—what was there to be nervous about?

He poured them both a glass and handed one to her. 'What shall we drink to?'

To us, she wanted to say—but only a fool would have made a toast as inappropriate as that. 'Let's drink to happiness.'

He wanted to wince but sipped his wine instead, before putting put his glass down to dig deep inside his pocket to produce a small packet. He held it out towards her.

Wide-eyed, Rebecca stared at it, and then up at him. It looked like… 'What's this?'

'Why not open it and see?'

A *present*? A present which looked awfully like *jewellery*? Carefully, she put her drink down and fumbled with the wrapping to reveal a pair of earrings. They were large amber ovals—simple and bright as syrup, set in plain silver—and she stared at them for a moment, her eyes blinking furiously because the gesture was so unexpected.

'Put them on,' he said.

They gleamed against her ears and reflected back the colour of her hair. 'Oh, Xandros—they're beautiful,' she breathed. 'But why have you bought me earrings?'

Something to remember me by. 'Isn't a man allowed to buy a woman presents?' he retorted softly.

'Well, yes, but…' A timer starter pinging in the kitchen. 'Damn!' she exclaimed. 'I'd better go and turn the oven off.'

'Leave it.'

'I can't leave it—the pie will burn.'

'Let it burn.' He snaked his hands around her waist and brought her up close to him, seeing the violet-blue light from her eyes darken with desire as he began to kiss her.

But for once Rebecca couldn't relax into it. Was that burning she could smell? After all her hard work? 'The dinner…'

He said something soft and explicit in Greek as she pulled away from him.

'Xandros, I must go and check the dinner.'

'Must you?'

His hand caressed her cheek and for a moment, she hesitated. She knew he wanted her, just as she wanted him—but this had to change. She had spent most of her last few days off making everything perfect for this evening—and just because he had bought her a beautiful present didn't mean that she should change all her plans and let everything spoil, did it?

'You've taken me out for so many meals that I want to treat *you* for a change,' she whispered as she traced his lips with the tip of her finger. 'I shan't be long.'

Moodily, Xandros waited while she clattered around with pots and pans. He could hear the sound of some kind of extractor fan sounding like a small aircraft about to take off in her kitchen. By the time she eventually returned and deposited dishes and plates on the table, her face was all warm with steam and tendrils of hair were spilling untidily around her face.

'It's a bit burned.'

'So I see.'

'Your fault for kissing me.'

'*Fault?*' he echoed faintly.

'Or mine for letting you.' But he didn't smile back.

They dished the meal out in silence and Rebecca couldn't shake off the terrible sense of impending doom as she gave him a portion of the least cremated part of the pie.

'So when did you last eat a home-cooked meal?'

He wanted to say never—and wouldn't that have been the truth? But Xandros had no desire to tell her that and to have to parry the questions which would inevitably follow.

And wasn't there one tiny part of him which couldn't fail to be touched by all the trouble she'd gone to tonight? But he steeled his heart against it— because he knew the category of this evening's entertainment.

It was: See *what a perfect home-maker I can be, Xandros.*

There were others, of course.

The: *Let me ensnare you with my sexual prowess, Xandros.*

Or, *I'll make myself so indispensable to your life that you'll wonder how you ever managed without me, Xandros.*

But they were all variations on a theme. All part of the games that women played. Show them a single man with sex appeal and billions in the bank and they seemed to go straight onto some kind of predictable autopilot. Xandros would be the last person to deny his own arrogance and self-assurance—but it was a simple fact that women had been trying to marry him for years.

Was that why Rebecca had produced this touching little scene tonight? Had she decided that a man so used to untold wealth would be captivated by a more humble setting? Didn't she realise that he had seen it all before—and then some more?

'Xandros?' she prompted him, hating the tense and forbidding mask which seemed to have tightened his handsome face. 'I was asking when you'd last had a home-cooked meal like this?'

He topped up their wineglasses and gave her a bland smile. 'I don't remember.'

Rebecca frowned. They never talked about the kind of stuff that other couples talked about. Surely they'd been together long enough now for her to be able to ask him a little more about his past? Because how could they get to know one another better without knowing the basics? 'What about when you were a little boy?' she asked, her voice growing gentle—trying to imagine him as a youngster.

'Was there something specific you wanted to know?' he questioned coolly.

'Well, not really *specific*—I meant more general, really.' She smiled at him in silent appeal. *I'm interested, that's all*—her eyes tried to tell him. 'You never talk much about your life in Greece, or your brother, for that matter. I can't even remember his name.'

He felt like pointing out that his brother's name was irrelevant. 'His name is Kyros. And there is nothing much to say. You know the facts about my former life.' His black eyes glittered her a warning. 'I left when I was eighteen and I have not been back.'

'But he—Kyros—he's your *twin*, isn't he?'

'And?' She was using his brother's name as if she knew him! As if she ever would! Xandros pushed his plate away and his eyes were cold—for she had persisted when he had made it very clear that he did not wish to pursue the subject.

'The world seems to have some kind of universal theory about twins which is based on sentiment rather than fact,' he ground out. 'The consensus being that there is always some kind of telepathy—some unbreakable bond between them. Well, let me tell you, Rebecca—that much is pure fantasy.' As were so many of the myths peddled about family lives. That mothers cared and fathers played with their sons.

She was taken aback by the sudden harshness in his voice, as if she had touched on a very raw nerve indeed. Intuition told her to back off, but a far more powerful instinct overrode it. Because what was the point of being with Xandros if all she was allowed to do was operate within the strict emotional boundaries he seemed to want to dictate? Hadn't that been one of the reasons why she'd organised this wretched dinner in the first place? To burrow beneath his peculiar icy-yet-passionate persona to find the real substance of the man beneath.

'You sound so bitter, Xandros,' she ventured quietly. 'So angry. Won't you tell me why?'

He flinched as if she had struck him, staring at her. 'You dare to call me bitter? You dare to speak of what you do not know?'

He was twisting her words, just as he was twisting his mouth into a contemptuous curve of condemnation. 'It wasn't meant like that!' she protested. 'It wasn't supposed to be an insult. All I wanted—'

'I don't care what you want!' he bit out. 'Because what *I* don't want is to unburden myself to you, my beauty.' Black eyes burned into her. 'That was never part of the deal.'

His words weren't making sense. 'The deal?' she echoed unsteadily. 'What deal?'

His heart had begun to pound, the blood to beat thickly through his veins. Draining off the last of his wine, he put the empty glass down on the table. 'My time with you was supposed to be a pleasant inter-lude—and now suddenly I'm supposed to be baring my soul just because you've peeled a few potatoes. If I'd wanted a damned therapy session I could have crossed the road in New York and found a hundred!' He saw her stricken face and with an effort, he quelled his fury. 'Listen, Rebecca,' he said, in as gentle a voice as he'd ever used with her. 'What we've had together has been—'

'Nothing!' cut in Rebecca furiously—because she saw where this was heading as clearly as if she were emerging from the darkness into the bright, glaring light of day. He was about to dump her! And along with that revelation came the realisation of just how weak and compliant she'd been all along—always ac-commodating *his* needs. It had been Xandros, Xandros, Xandros all the way. She had tiptoed around him, trying to gauge what *he* wanted and how *he* felt. She had walked on eggshells and look where it had got her. Suddenly, she felt filled with self-disgust at the way she had behaved.

So if she didn't like the way she had been treated by the Greek billionaire—then she had only herself to blame. It wasn't too late for her to seize the tattered remnants of her pride before he did irreversible damage to it. She sucked in a shuddering breath. 'You know—for all the fancy restaurants and beautiful hotels—it's really been nothing but sex and small talk! That's all we've ever had between us,' she bit out tremblingly. 'And do you know something else, Xandros? I'm glad it's over. Yes, *glad*!'

Xandros stilled, his senses on alert. 'But I haven't told you that it's over.'

Rebecca almost laughed out loud at his exquisite arrogance—if it hadn't already started to hurt so much. 'No, that's right. You haven't. Because I'm telling *you*. It's over—maybe it should never have begun. Heaven knows, I did my best to resist you.'

'But you couldn't,' he taunted.

'No. I couldn't. You're very good, Xandros—I'll admit that. The best, in fact. It would take a stronger woman than me to resist you and the charm you oozed all over me at the time—but which seems to have been in ever-diminishing quantities ever since.' Her eyes flashed him a challenge. 'But at least we both know now where we stand—so I think perhaps you'd better go, don't you?'

He saw the high flush of colour which washed over her cheekbones and the violet-blue fire which sparked from her eyes and in that moment he knew an overwhelming anger at her insolence and interference—coupled with a rush of desire so strong that he felt himself hardening against his will.

'Yes, I'll go,' he said, and God forgive him but he enjoyed the instinctive way she bit her lip at his ready agreement. She would live to regret her impetuosity! And yet he could not resist one parting shot—one more arrogant demonstration of how he could still pull the strings, should he so desire. 'But before I do—what about a farewell kiss?' he suggested, his voice one of deceptive silk. 'For old times' sake?'

'N-no.' But Rebecca's protest sounded half-hearted and it was too late anyway, for he had caught hold of her and was pulling her into his arms.

One touch and she was lost. Willingly lost. Like a line of fierce flame sweeping down an arid hillside—scorching everything in its touch with instant combustion. She heard his groan as he tightened his embrace and she heard her own echo it. *Please make me stop him,* she begged herself—but she made no move to stop him.

Afterwards, she would try to justify her actions by telling herself that it was like someone who was just about to go on a long journey without food or drink—and who could blame them for taking part in a banquet if it was offered?

But this was Xandros as she had never seen him before—like a pure-bred stallion, all excitement and fire. And his wild fervour only fuelled her own urgent need. She wanted to drown in his kiss and take him down with her. His hands were on her breasts, moulding them luxuriously against his palms, and then they were smoothing frantically down over her hips and her bottom—and he had begun to ruck her dress up like a man possessed.

And all the while he was kissing her—varying the kiss so that it was in turns hard, and then soft. Cajoling her and tempting her and then inciting her to touch him back—to run her fingers greedily over the hard ridge in his jeans, so that he gave a low, throaty laugh of pleasure.

'Unzip me,' he commanded roughly—and to her everlasting shame, she did just that.

Her expensive panties—which were new and had been bought especially for the seduction she had planned for later—were destined to be ripped off and allowed to flutter uselessly to the floor. She couldn't even in all conscience blame him, could she? Not when she was writhing around—so turned on that she thought she might have urged him to do just that.

There was no finesse about what was taking place now. Xandros was pushing her down against the hard floor and yet her arms were reaching up to try to pull him down on top of her. And he was groaning again, just yanking his jeans down, and she realised that he wasn't going to bother taking them off but was just going to…going to…

He let out a cry as he thrust into her and it was echoed by her own. She sobbed as he drove in deeper, and then deeper still—deeper than he had ever been—as if he were piercing her soul itself. The wild scream she let out as she bucked beneath him was the heralding of her orgasm—but it also signalled the breaking of her heart. Because the heart didn't respond to reason and—no matter how many reasons she threw at herself why she shouldn't—the fact was that she loved him.

She could feel the salty taste of tears welling up at the back of her throat as she tried to imagine a life without Xandros and it was like trying to conjure up a bleak, bare landscape with no sign of light on the horizon.

Afterwards, she lay there for as long as it took for his body to grow still, and then heavy. Hearing his breathing grow more steady, until she was sure that he must have fallen asleep. But then she felt him move.

Moving out of and then away from her and she kept her eyes tight closed to keep the tears at bay—hating herself for wanting him back in her arms, wishing that the whole stupid scene and row had never happened and they could have carried on with the evening as she had planned. Damn it—she couldn't even remember what the argument had been about.

Silently, Xandros rose to his feet, adjusting his clothes and zipping up his jeans, his heart still pounding madly in his chest. He stared down at Rebecca—her hair had come down and it spilled all over her rosy-flushed neck, shining gold against the rose. A stab of guilt pierced him as he noted the torn and discarded panties on the floor, until he reminded himself that she had wanted that just as much as him. Easily as much.

'Rebecca?'

She turned her face to the wall and the pain in her heart made her want to curl up like a broken animal. 'Just go, will you, Xandros?' she said wearily.

His eyes narrowed, capturing her and the scene in a brief snapshot to file away in his memory one last time. 'Goodbye, Rebecca,' he said softly, and shut the door very quietly behind him.

CHAPTER FIVE

'WOULD you mind coming in to see me, please, Rebecca?'

Vanessa's cool voice came down the line and Rebecca gripped the receiver with knuckles which were suddenly snow-white. 'But my flight isn't due to leave until this evening,' she protested.

'I know that. I have your flight schedule right here in front of me.' Vanessa's voice was now positively icy. 'And I'd really like to see you straight away.'

Rebecca stared at the phone—as if her boss were suddenly going to leap out of it and confront her here, in the supposed sanctuary of her own home, instead of demanding she turn up at the airfield hours early. But deep down, hadn't she been expecting a summons exactly like this?

The wonder of it was that it hadn't come sooner.

A lot had happened in the weeks since Xandros had walked out of her apartment after making love to her— and left her lying on the floor feeling cheap and used and heartbroken. She had crawled off to bed and sobbed as if her heart were breaking into a thousand pieces.

It had been a few days before she'd discovered that Xandros had stopped flying with Evolo airline—had terminated all his bookings abruptly and dramatically. The first she'd heard were Vanessa's mutterings of discontent in the office and Rebecca had prayed that her face wouldn't colour up and give away the fact that there might be a reason for his decision and that she was it.

But it had been a few weeks later that Rebecca made the most terrifying discovery of all. Even now she could scarcely believe it—but the doctor had confirmed it, and now she had to deal with it as best she could.

And how the hell is that going to be?

Grateful for the concealing uniform jacket, Rebecca pinned her already-too-tight work-skirt and slapped on far more make-up than usual as she prepared herself for the inevitable showdown. Didn't they say that make-up was a mask? And didn't she need some kind of camouflage to help her hide her true, see-sawing emotions of terror and despair?

Through the glass of her office, Rebecca could see Vanessa talking animatedly into the phone and when she glanced up and saw her a look of utter fury contorted her face. Putting the phone down, she beckoned to Rebecca to come in.

'Shut the door,' were her first words.

Rebecca pushed the door to. 'You wanted to see me,' she said, noting that Vanessa hadn't asked her to sit down, and she was left was standing there, like a naughty child who had been sent for by the angry head-teacher. *And isn't that accurate?* taunted the now-familiar voice of her guilty conscience. *Don't you deserve everything you're about to get?*

'Don't play the innocent with me, Rebecca,' said Vanessa coldly. 'You must realise exactly why you're here.'

How much did the steely blonde know? Rebecca played for time. 'I think—'

'No, that's the bloody problem—you didn't think, did you? You just let yourself get carried away and broke the cardinal rule of not sleeping with the clients!'

Vanessa's eyes narrowed into spitting shards and Rebecca thought that there was more to her rage than an employer's justifiable anger. Hadn't Xandros himself hinted that Vanessa had once made a pass at him? And hadn't he said it in the tone of a man for whom such behaviour was an occupational hazard? Rebecca flinched, wondering just who might be coming on to him now.

'I'm sorry,' she whispered.

'What the hell did you think was going to happen?' Vanessa cut off Rebecca's apology with a slicing movement of her perfectly manicured hand. 'Didn't you realise that people would notice you making cow's eyes at him, even though you were trying to hide it? Were you stupid enough to think there was some kind of future in it? Did you really think that a man like Alexandros Pavlidis was going to offer you anything other than a quick, convenient screw?'

'I…I don't have to listen to this, Vanessa.'

'Oh, but you do, Rebecca, you most certainly do. You've not just lost me one of my most prestigious customers—but all the possible associates he might have brought with him! The least you can do is hear me out!'

'But there's nothing left to say, is there?' asked Rebecca, her heart beating fast, intuition telling her that Vanessa still hadn't worked out the worst part of the whole situation.

'There's plenty to say!' stormed Vanessa. 'You've made my organisation look unprofessional and you've only helped to further ruin the reputation of cabin crew everywhere!'

'Look, I've said I'm sorry,' said Rebecca again. 'Really I am—but Xandros was so persistent...and I...I...'

But Vanessa's face went red with rage. 'Oh, was he? Well, in my experience men are never persistent unless they get the green light from a woman.' She slammed her pen down on the desk. 'And let me tell you something else—and that is that you'll never work in this industry again. I'll make sure of that. Now get out.'

There was one hazy segment of her mind which made Rebecca wonder if you could be kicked out on the street in this day and age. Until she reminded herself that what she had done would rightly be defined as gross misconduct, which *was* a sacking offence. And what would she prefer: to walk out of here now and never see anyone from Evolo again—or to work out her notice and *really* give them something to talk about?

'I'll have my uniform sent back,' she whispered.

'Dry-*cleaned*, if you please,' said Vanessa sharply.

All the way home, Rebecca felt like an alien who

had just landed from outer space and was masquerading as a human. As if she didn't belong—not anywhere. She needed someone to turn to, but who could you turn to at a time like this?

Her widowed mother had remarried and gone to live in Australia. How could she ring her up and say: *Mum, I'm going to have a baby with a man I never expect to see again?*

She couldn't possibly tell any of the friends she'd made through work, could she? Vanessa would probably accuse them of fraternising with the enemy and it might put their own jobs on the line. And although her two best girlfriends were always there for her, both were busy with their careers and neither of them lived in London. If they had done, then maybe her terrible news would have all come tumbling out over a cup of coffee—but the truth of it was that she felt oddly ill at ease about telling anyone.

Especially when you haven't even told the father!

Rebecca shivered. The hot August sun was beating down on her head, but inside she felt as if someone had replaced her blood with ice cubes as the undeniable words rattled round and round in her head.

I'm going to have a baby. That was the reality.

With no man, no job and no prospects. That was reality, too.

Rebecca stood stock-still as a red London bus swept by, the faces on it all blurred as one question kept going round and round in her head. What the hell was she going to do?

There weren't really a lot of options open to her.

Surreptitiously, her hand crept to her belly. It was

bigger, definitely bigger—but no one else had noticed. Not yet. Because Vanessa would surely have leapt on that if she'd thought that Rebecca was carrying Xandros's baby.

Xandros's baby. She shivered. Her Greek ex-lover was going to be a father and he didn't know. No one knew, but soon it would become all too apparent—and then what?

Then what?

She went home and carefully removed her uniform before putting on a summer dress—turning to look at herself from every angle in the mirror which stood in one corner of her tiny bedroom. The dress was filmy— it hinted at the body beneath instead of hugging it. To the uninformed eye, she looked just like a healthy and curvy young woman—with no clue to the new life which was growing within.

Among a clutter of bangles in a half-open drawer she caught a glimpse of something shiny. A stab of pain catching her unawares, she saw the silver and amber earrings which Xandros had given her that last, fateful night.

Had they been intended as a farewell gift? She thought so. In the end it had worked out differently from the way she suspected he must have planned it. Their relationship had ended dramatically—but the fact that it had finished hadn't come as a complete shock to her, had it?

But now there was a huge and lasting consequence to their liaison and she needed to be as grown-up about it as she had ever been in her life. Because Xandros might not have chosen to create a new life in those circumstances—she certainly wouldn't have done—but it was a done deal now. This baby existed and didn't he, as the father, have the *right* to know about it?

Of course he had a right. Rebecca had adored her own father—how terrible if she had been denied a relationship with him simply because he and her mother had not been together.

Yet deciding to tell him was one thing, actually doing it was another matter—especially after she had her twelve-week scan, when she knew that she really could not delay it for a second longer. A letter seemed so *impersonal*—and this was most definitely about a person. Several times she picked up the telephone and put it down again. How could you tell a man like Xandros something as momentous as this over the phone?

But it was more than that. A long-distance call could conceal so much, no matter how good the connection. And what if he refused to take her call—what then? Something was driving her on and she wasn't sure what it was, knowing that she wanted—no, *needed*—to see his face when she told him. Was it a perverse desire to see the truth in his eyes, no matter how hurtful—would that help free her from her feelings for him once and for all? Or just some need to take some control back in a life which seemed to have run off the rails in so many ways?

Once she'd made her mind up, Rebecca set things in motion very quickly—and somehow it was comforting to have things to occupy her. As if, by concentrating on the logistics of going to see him, it took her mind off the future. She booked her flight to New York, found a hotel and rang her mother.

'You might as well take a half-empty suitcase,' her mother said, on a very crackly line from New South Wales. 'The shopping in New York's supposed to be terrific value.'

'Yes, it is,' said Rebecca, trying to sound 'normal'. Yet shopping was the last thing she felt like doing— even though she supposed a sensible person might scour the stores for pregnancy clothes. But, inevitably, money was tight. She had signed on with a temp agency, and although they had been providing as many office jobs as she cared to do it didn't exactly pay her a fortune and she needed to hang onto every penny she could until she was no longer able to work.

Rebecca hadn't been to America for years—when she'd worked for Evolo she'd done mainly short-haul. But she loved flying and would normally have savoured the experience—had not the significance of her trip made her unable to sleep or to concentrate on any of the films on offer.

Now that she wasn't being paid for by the airline she discovered there was no such thing as a cheap hotel in the middle of the city and the small room she'd ended up with was clean, but soulless. There were fake flowers in a vase and an enormous TV dominating the limited space. But at least the shower worked and afterwards she felt one hundred per cent better.

She lay down, intending to shut her eyes just for a moment—but when she opened them again she realised that it had been a lot longer than that. The artificial light which was streaming in through the small window showed that she had been asleep for hours and a glance at her watch confirmed it. It was almost ten o'clock at night!

Rebecca's heart sank. She had been planning to go to Xandros's place of work and just ask to see him—without giving him time to think up some reason why he shouldn't. But now she could see that she hadn't really been thinking straight—or did she really think that a man in Xandros's position would be instantly accessible to the general public?

At Evolo, she had worked with enough powerful people to know that they were always protected. Whether it was night or whether it was day, she would still need Xandros to give his permission if she wanted to see him. There was no way she would ever have been able to burst in on him, unannounced—not unless she was planning to hang around the entrance to his offices like some tramp waiting for a handout. And how undignified would that be?

Rebecca flinched. Well, there was no way she was going to postpone the inevitable—not for a moment longer. The sooner she had done her duty, then the sooner she could go away.

But it's ten o'clock at night—what if he's with another woman?

Then she would just have to face up to it—because that, too would be reality.

Her hair was all rumpled where she'd slept on it while it was damp, but there was no time to redo it. And this wasn't some kind of beauty contest. Rebecca had very firmly banished from her heart and her mind the idea that Xandros would take one look at her and realise what a fool he'd been. Because life wasn't like that—and even if it was she had been growing her self-respect in the intervening weeks. And there was no way she wanted a man who treated her like a sexual commodity, the way Xandros had done—even if she had gone along with it at the time.

Applying only a little make-up, she tied her hair back and put on the floaty dress. Then she pulled her phone out and tapped out his number with a trembling finger.

It rang for so long she thought it was going to go straight to messages but at last there was a click, and he said in his distinctive accent, 'Yes?'

Her name must have come up on the screen because she heard the wariness in his voice and it made her want to weep. If only she could have put the phone down. But she couldn't. She sucked in a deep breath.

'Xandros? Hello, it's me. Rebecca. Am I disturbing you?'

He didn't answer that. Staring out at the bright glitter of lights on the skyline with narrowed eyes, Xandros thought how to respond to her question in a thousand different ways. He hadn't expected her to ring him—and he didn't particularly want her to. But his curiosity was aroused—and he wondered what had made her swallow her pride to get in touch with him. 'How are you, Rebecca?'

That was quite a difficult one to answer. 'I need to see you.'

Need? A pause. 'But I'm in New York.'

'Yes, I know. So am I.'

This time the pause was so long that Rebecca actually thought he might have hung up on her. To her surprise he didn't demand to know just what she was doing in New York—but maybe that shouldn't have surprised her. He was many things, but never predictable.

'Where exactly are you?' he questioned.

She read out the address from the top of the laminated room-service menu which was lying on the bedside table. 'Do you know it?'

Did he know it? Ah, the exquisite irony of life! Briefly, Xandros closed his eyes. He remembered staying in that self-same area when he'd first arrived in the city—presumably for the same cost-cutting reasons as her—and thinking how the fabled streets of New York were certainly not paved with gold. He had seen homeless people, and hungry ones, too. He recalled his sense of shock—and his determination, too—that one day he should conquer this great city. Within weeks, he had found himself a job to help support him through college—and had never been back there since. 'Can you come here?' he questioned silkily.

'Where?

'I'm in the office.'

Rebecca stifled her instinctive sigh of relief. At least he wasn't cosying up to whoever must have replaced her by now. 'That's late,' she commented.

His mouth hardened. He wanted to tell her that the hours he worked were none of her damned business. Why the hell was she here? Deliberately, he injected his voice with steel. 'I will send a car for you,' he said.

And the cool note in his voice reminded Rebecca of another stark reality of the situation. They were ex-lovers. There was no fondness for her in Xandros's heart. *And even less when he discovers what you are about to tell him.* 'No, I'll take the subway—'

'Don't be so ridiculous, Rebecca,' he cut in, with an impatient click of his tongue. 'It's late and I've said I'll send a car. The driver will ring you when he's outside.'

Rebecca recognised that there was no sense in arguing with him—and that to do so would be fairly stupid, under the circumstances. Why turn down his offer of safe transport in a strange city at night?

'Thanks,' she said, and put the phone down quickly.

And, besides, she was beginning to feel rather peculiar and she couldn't quite work out whether that was because she was pregnant or slightly jet-lagged or because she hadn't eaten since early on in the flight.

So eat something!

Her burgeoning body craved food and she had no desire to faint in front of him. Raiding the mini-bar like a guilty teenager, she ate chocolate, some pretzels and a glass of juice and worried how much they would charge her for the pleasure of eating junk. And then her phone began to ring and she felt a little like someone going to face their own trial.

A dark limousine was waiting outside with a uniformed driver holding open the door for her. She sat back on soft leather as the powerful car negotiated the streets—so new to her and yet strangely familiar from years of having seen them on TV programmes—but Rebecca wasn't really paying attention to them. She was too wrapped up in choosing her words as carefully as possible.

But how did you tell someone who was so definitely in your past that you were carrying part of his future?

The car stopped outside a vast, towering building lit mutedly save for the very top of it, which shone as brightly as a planet. A young woman stood waiting by the entrance, her tumble of dark curls and striking scarlet dress suddenly making Rebecca feel very pale and unexciting. Who was she? she wondered—hating herself for still caring as the brunette opened the car door.

'Hi. I'm Miriam.' The woman smiled, her teeth gleaming like a dentistry advertisement. 'Xandros asked me to come and meet you. He's upstairs in his office.'

'Thanks,' said Rebecca, feeling more than uptight now as a glass lift sped upwards. He hadn't come to fetch her himself, had he? And how, she wondered, had Xandros explained her sudden appearance to this woman Miriam? Was this his girlfriend—sent down to fetch her so that there could be no possible misunderstandings? Or was she a powerful man's gatekeeper—would she expect to sit in on what was probably going to be the most difficult conversation of Rebecca's entire life?

Well, she was going to have to assert herself. She was *not* going to have an audience while she stumbled to tell him. If he wanted he could tell Miriam later, once Rebecca had gone.

She was taken into a large and very beautiful office, dominated by a giant desk on which lay a few large sheets of drawings in various stages of development, and a pot full of pens and pencils. Apart from that, the room was completely bare of adornment—with no pictures on the walls or trinkets on his desk. At first, Rebecca didn't see Xandros, but then she sensed rather than heard him behind her and she turned to find him at the far end of the long room, watching her—and she could not help the instinctive shiver of awareness that felt midway between fear and desire.

'That will be all, Miriam,' he said.

Well, she didn't *sound* like a girlfriend. 'Is that your secretary?' asked Rebecca hopefully when the other woman had closed the door behind her.

'She's another architect, actually,' drawled Xandros, noticing her flinch at the unmistakably caustic note in his voice—but what did she expect? He had no idea why she was here today—whether it was all part of some sophisticated game-plan. Was that why she had jumped in and ended the relationship before he'd had a chance to do so? As a kind of emotional one-upman-ship—a clumsy effort to try to make him commit to her? But if so, it had backfired spectacularly—and she was just about to find that out.

She had made him feel…what? Trapped and irri-tated by her growing neediness and her desire to want to read all the secrets of his heart? Yet along with that he had felt oddly out of control, too. Hadn't it been a relief to be free of her strange, sensual power—even if he had found himself sometimes missing the passion of her embrace? Hadn't he terminated his contract with the airline because he had no wish for repeated contact with her or the temptation of her continuing allure? Those violet eyes and the silky hair like dark honey, which had trickled through his fingers so sweetly.

'Won't you sit down?'

'Thank you.' Despite the food she'd taken from the mini-bar Rebecca's knees were trembling and she sank into a leather chair with relief.

'You would like a drink? Some water, perhaps?'

She shook her head, feeling as if she were on a job interview—praying that her composure would not leave her at a time when she had never needed it more badly. 'No, thank you.'

Xandros stared at her, waiting for some kind of explanation for her appearance, but she had bent her head and was studying her clasped fingers intently— as if they were about to reveal something fascinating. And suddenly he was irritated. What the hell was she doing here? 'So?'

Rebecca looked up, braving herself to meet the expression on his face. How best to say it? The carefully chosen words she had been silently rehearsing on the way over suddenly seemed as inadequate as someone trying to staunch the flow of a burst dam using their finger. *There is no 'good' way to say this, Rebecca— so just say it.*

'I'm pregnant, Xandros.'

He didn't move, or react—grateful, if such a word could be used at such a time, for the enigmatic exterior which had never let him down.

Rebecca's voice wasn't quite steady as she searched his face. 'Did you hear me, Xandros? I said—'

'*Ne,* I heard you.' Inexplicably, he found himself thinking of Notus—the great south wind of Greece which brought with it the storms of summer and autumn—and what greater storm than this to have exploded in his life? A baby—by a woman who meant nothing to him? Yet still his face gave nothing away. Meeting her violet-blue eyes with nothing but stony question, he said: 'Are you certain?'

For one moment she wondered if she should draw his attention to the slight swelling of her belly until she remembered that she had come here because she had felt it was the *right* thing to do. She was not going to be made to feel the guilty party. He might not have planned this, but neither had she.

'Yes, I'm certain. I did a test and now the doctor has confirmed that they…' As his head jerked up she swallowed. 'Yes, they,' she whispered, meeting the blazing question in his black eyes. 'It's twins. I'm expecting twins, Xandros. Around the middle of January,' she finished hoarsely.

Twins. The word dropped into his consciousness like a stone falling into water from a great height and Xandros experienced a sensation of anger and pain so strong that it momentarily took his breath away.

Twins.

Hot, unwanted emotions washed over him—trying to take him back to a childhood he had buried and forgotten. A mother who had left him. A father who had never been there. A brother to whom he was joined for ever—whether he liked it or not. A brother he had fought with. Two men who had allowed time to deepen the rift between them.

Xandros scowled, recognising that in a way this was Rebecca's salvation—nature cleverly ensuring that he wouldn't question her about the paternity of her unborn. Yet for some reason that question had simply not occurred to him. Because her very neediness during their time together had convinced him that she would not have taken another lover—despite his occasional streak of jealousy? Or just his natural arrogance assuring him that it would be a long time before she would allow another man to touch her as he had touched her?

But the image disturbed him.

Twins.

He stared at her. 'You are quite sure of this?'

Did he think she was testing him out? Telling herself that it was shock which was making him snap the question out like an interrogator, Rebecca nodded.

'Yes. Testing procedures are very sophisticated these days. They can do a check between nine and—'

'That's enough!' He silenced her with an automatic raise of his hand, the imperious gesture telling her that he was simply not interested in the detail. That he needed time to think.

Xandros walked over to one of the large windows where the radiance of countless lights illuminated the night sky of New York, his adopted city. During the day, he sometimes went along the corridor to a smaller office where the light was soft and muted—because sometimes he found the urban magnificence of the skyline all too distracting, especially when he was working. But for now he welcomed the distraction from this momentous piece of news.

What the hell did a man do in a situation like this?

Eventually, he turned around. She hadn't moved

and her frame looked curiously fragile within the soft,
tooled leather of the chair. Her amazing hair was tied
back with a simple piece of ribbon and he thought that
she certainly hadn't gone to town on an outfit
designed to impress him. He saw the goose-bumps on
her slender arms and supposed that she wasn't really
used to the air-conditioning.

'*Say* something!' said Rebecca urgently, because
she could bear his brooding silence no longer.

'What do you want me to say, *agape mou*? That we
will all live happily ever after and that I will marry
you?' He gave a short, bitter laugh. 'Because I have
no intention of doing that.'

It hurt, of course it did—she would have had to have
been made of wood for it not to have done—but she
didn't react. One thing Rebecca had told herself was
that no matter what he threw at her, no matter *what* the
provocation—there was no way she was going to
storm out of here.

They would deal with this like adults—or rather *she*
would. So she kept her face as calm as possible instead
giving into the temptation of saying : *I wouldn't marry
you if you were the last man on earth!* She even
managed a shake of her head and a bland smile. After
all, she supposed that he could have denied paternity—and surely that would have been far more insult-
ing than him refusing to marry her?

'Marriage? Good heavens, no. That's not why I'm
here,' she said calmly.

'Really?' Ebony brows were elevated in thinly
veiled disbelief. 'Then why *are* you here?'

'Strange as it may seem, Xandros, it gives me no

pleasure to fly all the way over when I'm feeling slightly queasy and then be met with insult and accusation. I'm here because—as the father—I feel you have a right to know about it.'

For the first time he reacted outwardly, swearing softly and emphatically in his native tongue and it was her use of the word *father* which provoked it—because somehow that made it more real than the disconnected terms of babies and pregnancies. If his hands weren't his livelihood, he might have smashed his fist against one of the walls. But he lashed out with words instead.

'Okay, so you've told me. Pretty expensive and protracted way of doing so. You came all this way to tell me that? You didn't think of ringing?'

It would give too much away if she confessed that she'd wanted to see his expression when she told him. He might think she'd been holding out for a remarkable about-turn—as if he would pull her into his arms and tell her he'd missed her, and that having her carrying his babies beneath her heart was like a dream come true.

And hadn't there been a tiny part of her which hadn't ruled out that thought—even though it had flown in the face of all logic? That the man who had everything might realise that none of it mattered when compared to these miraculous new lives they'd created? But there could be no mistaking the lack of emotion on his proud and beautiful features. She had wanted an answer to her silent question and it was written there—in stark detail.

Slowly, Rebecca began to rise to her feet, her heart suddenly heavy.

'Where do you think you're going?' he demanded.

'Home. Well, back to the hotel. I have done what I came for.'

His black eyes narrowed. 'But nothing has been decided.'

'There's nothing *to* decide, Xandros. That isn't why I'm here. You are now in full possession of the facts and my conscience is clear.'

'Well, mine is not!' he thundered. He raked his fingers back through his ebony hair. 'I will pay!' he announced.

For a moment she completely misinterpreted what he meant and her trembling hand shot out to grab hold of the chair-back. '*P-pay?* What are you talking about?'

He stilled. 'What do you think? For your upkeep. For the children's—' Briefly, the word froze in his throat. 'For their upkeep, once they are born,' he continued. 'And you will need money to support yourself until that happens. I assume you won't be allowed to fly after a certain point? Isn't that what usually happens?'

She opened her mouth to tell him that she was not allowed to fly *now*—that she had lost her job because she had broken the rules—but did she want to come across as some kind of victim? No, she did not. In fact, it was imperative that she didn't. From now on she needed to be strong *and* independent—not just for her own sake, but, more importantly, for the sake of her babies. Babies. Rebecca shivered. If the idea of twins had come as a shock to Xandros, it had troubled her even more. He was used to two of everything, while she was a complete novice. How on earth was she going to manage?

'I didn't come here to ask you for money,' she said.

'Maybe not, but I am a wealthy man—we both know that.' His black eyes glittered. 'I want you to take what I am offering. In fact, I *insist* upon it.'

And as Rebecca looked into his eyes she realised that Xandros *needed* to give her something concrete— like money. That way he could wash his hands of all responsibility. Because he hadn't expressed the wish she had secretly prayed for—to want to play some part, no matter how small, in his children's lives.

She shook her head. 'You aren't in any position to insist on anything, Xandros,' she said.

Fleetingly, he thought it ironic that, with Rebecca in this new and physically vulnerable state, he had never seen her look or sound quite so strong and focussed. But maybe this was what she had wanted all along, despite her protests—something to tie her to him.

'But this is not a battle of wills, Rebecca,' he said softly. 'It is what is known as making the most of a bad situation. You live in that tiny place, which some might consider too small even for one. How the hell do you expect to be able to cope with, not one, but *two* new babies there—had you thought about that?'

'What do you think?' She had thought of little else. This would be a good cue for hysteria, Rebecca thought as she stared at him in disbelief—but she could not allow herself the indulgence of such a useless emotion. She registered the critical way he had dismissed her apartment. To think how hard she'd worked on it—hoping to impress him with her little home—and all the time he had felt nothing but contempt for it! Didn't he realise that not everyone was as fortunate as he was?

But it was her sheer short-sightedness which troubled her most. That she could have made so bad a judgement about a man. How could she have possibly thought that she loved him—when he had a heart of stone which made a mockery of the hard warmth of his body?

Rubbing her shivery arms with her hands and wishing she'd brought some kind of jacket, she fixed him with a look which told him that, although her self-respect might have taken a bit of a battering, she would repair it as best she could, but without any help from *him*.

'I'll manage somehow,' she said, her voice low but dignified. 'I may not be rich, but you can be sure that I'll love these babies, Xandros. I'll love them with all my heart—and I don't want anything from you. Do you understand that?'

His eyes narrowed as they met in a silent clash with hers, but unexpectedly her fervent words pierced him. She had said that she would love them—but he knew only too well that being a mother did not guarantee loving your children. When she realised that he meant what he said about not marrying her—would she still feel the same? Or might she then see adoption as a sensible solution?

'I understand perfectly,' he said. 'But whether you want help or not, you're getting it. I will pay money into an account for you—what you choose to do with it is up to you. In return, I ask that you keep me informed of your progress during the pregnancy. Is that understood?'

She stared at him. 'You mean you want to be involved?'

He hardened his heart against her violet eyes. 'I meant I want a progress report,' he said, as if he were talking about the construction of one of his own projects. 'I wish to know when they…' He swallowed then, despite his determination to feel nothing. 'I want to know when you give birth. Will you do that for me?'

'Yes.' The word was little more than a lost sigh in that great big office space and Rebecca stood up. If she didn't feel so emotionally and physically vulnerable, she would have left quietly and gone in search of the nearest subway. But she couldn't face it. 'I'd like to go now,' she said, in a low voice. Before she did something unforgivable, like breaking down into a cascade of choking sobs in front of him.

Xandros could see the trembling of her lips. Once he would have kissed that tremble away, but now he could not—for that would dishonour them both. Their relationship was over—they both knew that.

He suspected what she really wanted of him—what was probably expected of him—but he could not give any kind of emotional commitment to these unborn children. Far better to promise nothing than to fail to deliver. And didn't he come from exactly the right kind of background to walk away from a child? Didn't abandonment run deep in his veins?

Hidden by the shafts of his powerful thighs, his fists clenched in anger. 'My driver is waiting,' he said tightly. 'I will take you down to him.'

CHAPTER SIX

Yet for the first time in his life, Alexandros Pavlidis found himself proved wrong.

He had expected—what? That Rebecca would use her pregnancy to gain increased access to his life, in an attempt to make herself a permanent fixture there, no matter how much she had protested otherwise?

Yes, of course he had. Too often in the past women had lied to him or tried to conceal their true motives in their attempts to ensnare him. And didn't she have a more valid reason than any of her predecessors to want him in her life? Two babies on the way. Two babies which were due to be born in a few short weeks' time, according to the calendar on his kitchen wall.

Xandros finished knotting his silk tie and stared back at his image in the mirror. His eyes looked shadowed, his hard face unsmiling. In the frantic world beyond his condominium, a snowy New York was rushing to prepare itself for the holiday season, and no city did it better.

The giant Christmas tree at the Rockefeller centre was blazing with coloured lights and the ice-rink was filled with happy skaters. Department store windows were groaning with nostalgic images which had been lifted straight from the pages of children's books. On Xandros's mantelpiece, dozens of invitations were stacked like giant playing cards—but he was distracted.

Just what the hell was Rebecca playing at?

He had expected the generous allowance he had paid into an account for her to be withdrawn immediately, but he had been wrong.

He had expected regular updates from her—an attempt to involve him in the pregnancy with an excess of detail. Again, he had been wrong.

She had withdrawn no money—not a cent—and the only real news he had received about the pregnancy had been the two images from one of her scans. They had arrived in a plain brown envelope, marked 'Private and Confidential' and Xandros had sat staring at them for a long time.

He was used to studying pictures; that was part of his job—to see something grow from a rough design into something real—but this was something completely outside his experience.

At first his untrained eye could hardly distinguish between the grainy components of the photo, but gradually—like one of those optical illusions which people sent out over the internet—the image became clear. Yet it was still difficult to believe the import of what he was seeing. Were these tiny, tadpole-like shapes really potential human beings?

In spite of his determination not to think of the bigger picture, he felt a sensation which was midway between wonder and pain and, giving into rare impulse, he picked up the phone and dialled her number in England.

Her voice sounded wary. 'Hello?'

'It's me. Xandros.'

Yes, I know it's you, thought Rebecca and sucked in an unsteady breath. 'Hello, Xandros.'

It wasn't the most rapturous welcome in the world. Xandros stared out at the lightening New York sky and his mouth tightened. 'I called to see how you were doing.'

Give him the facts, Rebecca told herself. *Just the facts—that's all he wants.* 'Oh, the doctors are very pleased with my progress. The pregnancy is going exactly as it should and the babies—' How bizarre it felt to be saying this—to be discussing these intimate details with a man who felt little more than a stranger. Who *was* little more than a stranger. 'The babies are doing fine—so they tell me, looking at the scan. Did you get the pictures I sent you?'

In spite of his determination not to react, Xandros felt his heartbeat increase. When she said 'babies' like that—in that soft, English accent—it sounded frighteningly real and yet ridiculously far-away. 'Yes. Yes, I got them. What are you doing for Christmas?'

She had told herself to expect nothing, but she had absolutely no control over the sudden hopeful lurching of her heart. Did he realise that she was pretty much trapped by size and circumstance? But if she told him the truth—that she was planning to overdose on choco-late and sloppy films—wouldn't that sound as if she were some poor little victim, desperate for her white knight to come along and scoop her up on his charger. Well, Xandros was certainly no white knight—and she was certainly no victim.

'Oh, I'm being very lazy,' she said, injecting as much purring satisfaction into her voice as she could. 'What about you?'

He thought of all the parties he'd been invited to and the people who would be at them—the über-thin women, so eager to please and to take him to their beds. The Park Avenue matrons so keen to marry off their daughters—his power and Greek virility in exchange for some obscene trust fund. But suddenly Rebecca's satisfied voice became the main focus in his mind and he felt the first simmerings of annoyance.

Because her response wasn't what he had been expecting, either. Shouldn't there have been a wistful little note in her voice—as if she was wishing or hoping that things could have been different between them? As if ideally she would like to have been curled up in front of a holiday fire with him?

'Oh, the usual festive revelry,' he said carelessly as he ran his fingertips over one thick, gold-embossed card. 'More invitations than I can cope with. You know what it's like.'

She didn't, of course—but Xandros wasn't aware of that and nor did he need to know how isolated her life had become. Maybe cocooning herself away as much as possible was nature's way of ensuring that she got all the rest her tired body was craving.

She had been accepted by the others in her antenatal classes—they were really sweet—even though she was the only single mother in a group of ecstatic couples. They all wanted to fuss round her because she was expecting twins—Rebecca didn't mind that bit at all—but some protective instinct had made her deflect their curious questions.

Maybe she was wrong, but she found herself unwilling to tell them her story—for wouldn't it sound as if she'd foolishly reached for the stars and then come crashing down to earth?

I fell in love with a Greek billionaire and after we'd finished I discovered I was pregnant.

Why, even to her *own* ears she sounded like some kind of gold-digger!

'Was there anything else you wanted, Xandros? I really have to go.' Before his clever tongue could cut through the precarious façade she had erected around her emotions and have her bursting into stupid tears.

Fingertip halting on the gleaming but unexpectedly sharp card edge, Xandros narrowed his eyes. 'You are alone?'

'I beg your pardon?'

'You have a man with you, perhaps?'

Rebecca gripped at the receiver. If she weren't so appalled at his amazing cheek, she might actually laugh aloud at his unmatchable arrogance. 'I don't know if you've seen a woman in the late stages of a twin pregnancy,' she snapped. 'I might even be flattered that you should consider me alluring enough to attract a man in such a condition—if it were any of your business, but it's not. I'm a free agent, Xandros— you don't have any rights or any say in what I do. So if that's all, I'm going to hang up.' She drew in a deep breath. 'Oh, and don't worry—I'll text you and let you know when I go into labour. Goodbye.'

It took a moment for Xandros to realise that she had actually done as she threatened and terminated the conversation! And another for him to process what she'd said to him. She had told him that he had *no rights* over her. In fact, she had not told him—she had snapped the information out, like a woman who was clearly impatient to get away.

He had never heard her talk that way before. She always used to work around his mood, and, even though it had irritated the hell out of him at the time, he wasn't certain that he approved of this new, feisty Rebecca either.

And she would 'text him' about the birth, would she? *Text* him? Moodily, he stared at the party invite. Since when was such news relayed in such a casual manner?

He worked late at the office and afterwards went to a dinner—mainly because it was just around the corner on Lexington. It was a beautiful apartment and a beautiful party by anyone's standards—even those as exacting as Xandros's. A huge penthouse room was lit by tall candles and scented with waxy white flowers—a stark black Christmas tree decked only in white, glittering baubles.

Everything matched. Nothing out of place. As uncluttered as it was possible to be. It looked like a film-set—or an advertisement for how the rich really lived. And they really did live like this, thought Xandros.

A classical pianist played on a white grand piano and the hostess, who was newly divorced and young enough to consider Xandros a serious bet, was dressed in a shimmering white gown which clung to every sensuous curve of her body.

'Hello, Alexandros,' she drawled, in her soft Southern accent. 'You look so bushed I think I might send you straight to bed.' Her voice dipped. 'And if you're very lucky—I might join you.'

'Time I was leaving,' he said brutally.

'Oh!' She laid light, fleeting polished fingernails on his suit jacket as he waved away a glass of champagne. Xandros imagined those gleaming nails touching his bare skin and he shuddered in distaste, wondering why he'd come here.

Because you wanted to forget.

Forget what? The fact that he was soon to be a father and nobody knew about it. A fact so bizarre that he was having difficulty believing it himself.

The text came in the middle of his night—though it would have been Rebecca's morning—the day after Christmas. That strange, flat day following the holiday itself. The text was spare with detail, saying simply: 'In labour. Will let you know what happens.'

What the hell did she think was going to happen? he wondered.

But after that he couldn't sleep, pacing the floor of his apartment, trying to settle with a book, a film and then some music—but nothing worked. Obviously, he knew nothing about childbirth except what he'd seen depicted in movies—when the women always seemed to scream and thrash around a lot. Was that dramatic licence, or was Rebecca screaming out in pain right now?

Xandros gritted his teeth because somehow that hurt. And the not knowing anything was the worst feeling he could recall in a long time. He was a man of action—he did not think, he *did*. So was he going to sit around now and wonder what the hell was going on across the Atlantic—or was he actually going to do something about it?

His bag was packed in seconds, a flight arranged and a car dispatched to take him to JFK for the first flight to London. Xandros never rejoiced in money for money's sake, but it was at times like this that he recognised the true freedom that his wealth could buy him.

It was a bleak day when he touched down at Heathrow—the sky was heavy and overcast and there was an air of chill which made steam clouds of his breath. He had texted Rebecca right back and asked her which hospital she was going to and she had told him. He guessed she presumed he'd want to send flowers or something. He had not told her he was coming.

Why not?

Because he had not wanted to risk her objecting? Knowing that even a man as macho as he was would have baulked at overriding a woman's wishes while she was actually in labour?

Or because he had wanted to check out that she'd spoken the truth when she'd implied that there was no man in her life? She might have protested about her physical state but Xandros was enough of a cynic to realise that someone with an eye for the main chance might jump at the opportunity of hooking up with a beautiful woman—especially if there was going to be some super-rich ex-lover in the background, paying her bills.

The message came through when he was almost at the hospital.

Two healthy babies...

And then, infuriatingly—*some text missing.*

So were they boys, or were they girls? Or were they one of each? Striding in through the glass doors of the maternity unit, he told himself that it didn't matter what sex they were. Several nurses asked if they could help him—one in particular looking as though she wasn't talking about directions—and soon he was in the maternity unit, speaking to the nurse in charge.

'I'm looking for Rebecca Gibbs,' he stated.

'And you are?'

Who the hell do you think I am? 'I'm the babies' father. Alexandros Pavlidis,' he bit out. 'Where is she?'

'Please follow me, Mr Pavlidis—and I'll take you to her.'

Rebecca was lying on a bed, feeling as if she were in some kind of drugged daze—though in truth she'd only puffed at a bit of gas and air because that had been all there'd been time for during a labour which had taken her by surprise with its speed and intensity. But now, with the pain and the ordeal part of it over, she was drifting in and out of a strange kind of half-sleep when a familiar accent prickled over her senses and convinced her that she must be dreaming.

'Rebecca?'

She opened her eyes, screwed them up—as if it

might be a trick of the light and the hard, handsome face of her ex-lover weren't towering over her like some dark, avenging angel.

'Xandros?'

'Where are they?' he demanded.

The midwife made as if to object at his tone, but weakly Rebecca shook her head. She wanted to cry. 'Over there,' she whispered.

Slowly, he turned and walked towards two cribs which stood, side by side, an identical swaddled shape in each—a shock of black hair the only contrast against the white hospital blanket. He felt a shiver whispering its way over his skin, his throat growing dry as he stared down at them.

'What are they?' he questioned thickly.

For a moment Rebecca didn't understand him—until she realised that he still didn't know the sex. She paused, as if recognising the significance of what she was about to tell him—resenting it even as she resented the stupid pride she felt in the answer she was about to give him.

'Boys,' she answered. 'Both boys.'

'Identical?'

'Yes, Xandros.'

Xandros closed his eyes as the turbulent reality of what she had just told him rocked him to the very core of his being—for it was every Greek man's dream to have a son to carry on his name and his genes. But *twin* boys? Just like him and Kyros. The cell split into two. The same and yet not the same. Never the same. Would any other man understand this strange bond of twinship, which now reached down through another generation?

For a moment he was shaken. More than shaken. He felt the strange thunder of his heart as he stared down at the two ebony heads and a terrible tearing at his heart as if someone had just ripped it open.

'Would you like to hold your sons, Mr Pavlidis?' asked the midwife with the bright, forced emotion of someone who had asked that particular question a million times.

Xandros looked up, and for a second his intense black gaze burned into Rebecca with an expression which came as close to helpless as she could ever imagine Xandros looking.

'You mean, both of them?'

Rebecca actually smiled. 'Well, why don't you start with one, and see how you go on?'

Did he begrudge her apparent serenity—or was it simply that he felt as uncertain as some of the novice skaters he'd seen on the Rockefeller ice rink as he tentatively looked down at the tiny bundle, which seemed to be making sucking sounds disproportionate to his tiny size. 'Why not?' he questioned, and held his arms out.

The midwife bent down and efficiently scooped one of the babies up, before placing him in Xandros's arms. 'Make sure you support his little neck,' she said, in a friendly, bossy manner.

Xandros nodded, a lump forming in his throat as he cradled the scrap of an infant. How could this be? he wondered. This double miracle which had been created. *'Oyos,'* said Xandros softly, beginning to cradle him now. 'My son.'

Rebecca swallowed as she heard the primitive note

of ownership in his deep voice—telling herself that her fears were irrational. Shouldn't she be pleased that he had acknowledged his offspring so openly? Why, she hadn't expected him to turn up here like this. He hadn't warned her.

In her more vulnerable state during the pregnancy—during some of the long, restless nights when she couldn't get comfortable—hadn't she longed for just such a scenario? Xandros appearing out of the blue—all strong and unashamedly masculine. Xandros sweeping in to take over and transform the situation—as if he were possessed of magical powers and could sprinkle her world with stardust.

But that had been then—when Rebecca was feeling all mixed-up and weary with the weight of impending birth. Something had happened in the interim which seemed to have invested her with the magical powers she had foolishly expected Xandros to bestow upon her.

She had become a mother. She had two tiny babies who were dependent on her. It should have scared the life out of her, but somehow it did the very opposite—it filled her with a kind of strength unlike anything she'd ever felt before. The strength to be able to stand up to a man—even one as dominating as Xandros.

'Why didn't you tell me you were coming?' she questioned.

He looked up from where his lips seemed to have drifted automatically to the silken down of the baby's head. 'I wanted to surprise you.'

'Or to check up on me?' she questioned astutely.

The midwife frowned, as if interpreting the beginnings of a row. 'You are supposed to be resting—'

'Oh, I will ensure she rests,' Xandros cut in with a soft arrogance. 'And please—we must no longer keep you from your work. I should like a little time alone with the mother of my sons.'

Rebecca wanted to lash out—to tell him that decisions to rest or not to rest were down to *her*. And to protest at his rather cold-blooded description of her, which made her sound like little more than an incubator. But she did not want a scene. She could already sense that the midwife was on Xandros's side—if the slightly awestruck look she was giving him as she left the room was anything to go by. And more than that, she felt weak—physically shattered, as if she had gone ten rounds in a boxing ring and emerged punch-drunk.

She stared at his powerful dark form and realised that she needed to rest. That being strong was one thing—but who could say how long she'd be able to remain like that?

'Perhaps you'd like to come back later, Xandros?' she questioned, forcing her voice to sound polite, as if he was nothing to her. *Because he is nothing to you.* He might be the father of her two new sons, but that did not mean there was anything left between them and she would be a fool to forget that.

He was still staring at their tiny, sleeping forms. 'Have you thought of names?' he demanded, as if she hadn't spoken.

Of course she had thought of names—there had been plenty of thinking times during the long winter evenings when her bump had seemed to defy gravity and made moving around both difficult and uncomfortable. But it was hard enough choosing *one* name—

let alone two. And there had been no one to bounce ideas off. No one to say, 'I hate that name' which was what the giggling couples at the antenatal classes used to say.

And it had been difficult to imagine that the long, unplanned pregnancy would actually result in two little babies—even though every scan had confirmed that to be the case. But your mind could know something and your heart would refuse to accept it. It had felt like tempting fate to think ahead. To try to picture what the reality might be like. The doctors had fussed over her as it was—with a kind of fascinated horror. They had told her to take extra care and then had frowned with concern when she had told them that there was no father on the scene.

Would Xandros have come to her aid if she had told him she needed him during those months? Rebecca didn't know and neither had she wanted to test it out. She really *hadn't* wanted to see him. It would have stirred up unwanted emotions at a time when she had needed to keep all her sanity and her wits about her. And she had made a decision after her trip to New York—when he had made her feel like some inconsequential part of his former life. He had seen her vulnerable too many times in the past—and he would never see her vulnerable again.

'Perhaps you would like me to draw up a list of names?' he was asking, as if he had every right to do so.

Too tired after a long labour and taken aback by the unexpected visit, Rebecca was not in the mood for a fight—and, besides, surely they could manage to agree on something they both liked? She liked *his* name, didn't she? 'Yes, why don't you do that—unless you have any immediate suggestions?' she said wryly. 'Like Alexandros I and Alexandros II.'

But it seemed that Xandros was no longer listening. To her astonishment—he was carefully replacing the baby in his crib and then bending down to pick up the second child. Rebecca stared in a kind of dazed disbelief at the contrast it made. How could such a large and powerful man adapt so quickly and skilfully to handling such little newborns? She felt her heart give a little wrench of pain at the thought of all it could have been—and never would.

'You seem…you seem a remarkably quick learner,' she said shakily.

'*Ne*. All my life I have learned quickly,' he said, in a matter-of-fact way. Xandros touched a gentle finger to the soft cheek of the infant. Soon he would begin to learn their individual faces and, though other people might claim that they looked exactly the same, he would know differently.

A tell-tale crumpling of the mouth. The way that one nose cast a certain shadow which the other did not, and which only the most discerning eye would notice. When you were born an identical twin, you spent your lifetime searching for differences, rather than similarities. He would know these two babies apart within days.

The baby in his arms began to squawk and, as if by reflex, Rebecca felt the sudden heavy aching in her breasts and she held her arms out. 'He needs feeding,' she said awkwardly, her cheeks growing pink—which seemed bizarre under the circumstances. This, after all, was a man who knew her breasts better than anyone—so why was she suddenly feeling as shy as if there were a stranger standing in the room?

Xandros narrowed his eyes and then carefully bent down and handed the infant over to her. And for the first time he really looked at Rebecca as she began to move the nightgown aside and latch the baby onto her breast with fingers which still seemed a little hesitant about this new part of her life.

Her cheeks were all flushed and her honeyed hair had been caught back in a blue ribbon, though silken strands of it were falling down. And she was suckling his child. Had not that same breast borne the imprint of *his* mouth? Had she not cried out with pleasure when it had done so?

A fierce shaft of something he didn't recognise rocked him. Was it the shock of seeing her as a mother—the mother of *his* children—rather than simply as a sexually desirable woman?

His hard mouth twisted as he turned away from the picture-perfect image. Because things were never as they appeared. Never. Didn't he know that better than anyone?

He walked over to stare at the other infant, who had begun to stir. What if they both wanted feeding at the same time? How the hell would she be able to manage that? He turned back to find Rebecca watching him, her violet-blue eyes dark.

'You will bottle-feed them, I suppose?' He spoke with the tone of a man entering unfamiliar territory and for Xandros it was as close as he had ever come to hesitation.

Rebecca shook her head. 'I'm planning to continue nursing them myself.'

He was surprised, though he did not say so. The wives of his friends and colleagues had mostly abandoned their breast-feeding—mainly because they either had their careers or social lives to return to—but apparently it also did little to enhance the appearance of the breasts. Xandros remembered the genuine shock he'd experienced when a woman had informed him that her breasts had been surgically 'enhanced' and that she was therefore unable to feed her child. It had seemed the price she had been willing to pay for keeping a pert figure.

'You will manage two babies?' he questioned.

'Well, nature has equipped me to do that at least,' she said wryly. 'Just imagine if I'd had triplets!'

Unbelievably, he found his lips curving into a smile and suddenly he found himself wanting to get away from this uncomfortably intimate scene—and at the same time strangely reluctant to leave. Was that nature—that powerful and ungovernable force—exerting her strong will to pull him towards his sons?

'When will you be discharged?' he questioned.

Rebecca delayed answering—but she could hardly lie about it, could she? Or demand to know what business it was of his? She had *made* it his business when she'd told him about the pregnancy, and that decision—like everything else in life—had its consequences. Whether she liked those consequences was neither here nor there.

She would provide him with facts, pure and simple—beyond that she owed him nothing.

'After three days, hopefully,' she said. 'Provided that they're pleased with mine and the boys' progress, of course.'

He registered the ways she'd said *the boys*—like an exclusive little club which he was not permitted to join, and Xandros felt his body prickle its silent objection to her high-handedness. *We'll see about that,* he thought grimly.

He nodded. 'I will come and collect you,' he stated.

'But, I don't need—'

'Yes, you do. I'm not arguing with you, Rebecca—because there is no alternative.' His implacable words cut through her protest. 'I will be taking you all home from hospital and that is final.' His black eyes glittered with sudden, new intent. 'And now we need to discuss the names of my sons.'

CHAPTER SEVEN

'I DO not care what you say!' Xandros stormed. 'You cannot possibly stay here—and what is more, I will not let you!'

Rebecca sighed. If she'd had the energy she might have objected to the condemnatory tone of his voice—just as she might have objected to him standing there, dominating the sitting room of her little flat as he seemed to dominate every place he went.

Wishing he would go away—because he was so damned...so damned *everything*. Single-minded, stubborn...and gorgeous. So gorgeous. And she must never forget the power of his sexuality—no matter how many times she told herself that it was no longer relevant to either of them. Because he would use it as a weapon if he needed to, she recognised weakly. He would do anything he needed to do to get his own way.

In the end she had been pathetically grateful for his insistence that he collect her, Alexius and Andreas from the hospital. In fact, she wondered how on earth she could have managed without him. She literally *couldn't* have carried the two babies along with all her hospital stuff *and* managed even something as simple as opening the front door with a key which had always gone stiffly into the lock, but which had never seemed to matter until now.

As it was, on several occasions she'd had to bite back tears of frustration—telling herself that her emotions were only see-sawing all over the place because of her fluctuating hormone levels and the fact that she had recently given birth.

Xandros had organised a car, which she had accepted, and he had also offered to bring along a maternity nurse, which she had refused. That had vexed him, as had so much else—but nothing had irked him quite so much as looking round at her tiny home now that it had acquired two extra small human beings, along with all their assorted paraphernalia. There were giant, ugly plastic bags of nappies—and bottles of baby bath and packets of baby wipes. Why did everything have to be made out of plastic? he had wondered sourly more than once.

'Look at it!' he raged. 'You cannot possibly stay here!'

'I don't have any alternative,' said Rebecca. 'Lots of babies are brought home to places like this.'

'Not usually *two* babies at the same time! How the hell are you going to manage?' he demanded.

'I'll manage,' she said tiredly.

'You had enough difficulty getting back from hospital,' he pointed out. 'And you might just about cope with the babies since that is what nature has equipped you to do, as you keep telling me—but what about you? There is very little food in the fridge—and no fresh fruit or vegetables at all! It is outrageous!'

'We can't all have fleets of servants at our beck and call,' she said flippantly, in an effort to hide the hurt. 'Perhaps you'd like to do a quick supermarket shop for me?'

'Oh, I can do better than that,' he said grimly, sliding the phone from his pocket.

Within the hour, one of London's most chi-chi stores had delivered the kind of food which Rebecca could never have afforded, not even at Christmas, and for the first time in years, Xandros found himself unpacking it himself—and using every one of his spatial skills to try to fit most of it into her shoebox of a fridge.

He heated them both some soup and gave Rebecca some fruit juice while he drank a glass of wine and then watched as she fed the babies again. He cleared their supper away while she changed them—because his macho Greekness rebelled at *that*. As it was, it had been many years since he had washed dishes—and in a funny kind of way, he enjoyed it.

But when he walked back into the sitting room, he could see the exhaustion which had made her face paper-pale and the shadows underneath her eyes nearly as violet dark as her eyes—and never had he felt so…ineffective.

'You're tired,' he observed.

'Yes, I am. Thank you for all your help, Xandros—and I'll see you soon.'

He heard the dismissal in her voice and his mouth twisted into an odd kind of smile. 'Oh, but it isn't over yet, *agape*,' he said grimly. 'Because I am not going anywhere.'

'Wh-what are you talking about?'

'I shall sleep on the sofa tonight.'

She stared at him in alarm. 'But you can't!'

'Can't? Did you really imagine for one second that I would leave you here alone on your first night back at home—with two tiny babies? What if something happens to you? What if you should suddenly get sick?'

His protectiveness made her want to weep with a terrible kind of yearning—as she couldn't help but imagine how it would feel if his words were inspired by love, rather than paternal duty. But that was selfish, wasn't it? Her own fiery dreams of love with Xandros lay in ashes—but she must rise above all that and do the best for Alexius and Andreas. They both owed them that.

'I'll find you a duvet,' she said awkwardly.

'Thank you.'

Xandros could never remember spending such an uncomfortable night—not even when he used to sleep on the beach under the stars, on those balmy nights back in Greece, when the air had been so thick and so warm that it had been impossible to stay inside.

But back then he had been a teenager, his still-growing body adaptable to just about anything. In the intervening years he had become a man used to only the very finest things.

So should he be grateful for this opportunity to remind him of what life could be like for others less fortunate?

By morning, there was no question of gratitude. He had barely slept a wink—woken up by a dust-cart outside the window, which had seemed determined to give him the entire repertoire of its noisy engine, and then by the sound of rain beginning to thunder down.

For a while, he lay staring at his surroundings in a kind of dazed disbelief until he could hear the sound of Rebecca moving around and so he washed and dressed, and made coffee for them both. But the delicious smell of it did little to soothe his frayed nerves—serving only to remind him how this situation could not be allowed to continue.

He heard her footsteps and turned round as she came into the sitting room. She had tied her hair into two thick plaits, which hung down by the sides of her unmade-up face, and she was wearing a simple pair of linen trousers and a pale T-shirt. He thought how ridiculously young she looked, and oddly wholesome, too—and while wholesome was not a word he usually liked or associated with his women, perhaps it was the best to be hoped for under these particular circumstances.

'How did you sleep?' she asked, thinking how he seemed to dominate the room with his presence and how unsettling it had been to imagine him sleeping on the other side of the paper-thin walls.

'How do you think I slept?' he grated.

'I did try to warn you—'

'You are missing the point, Rebecca.'

He was *not* going to intimidate her in her own home. 'And what point is that, Xandros?'

'I told you yesterday—you can't possibly live like this!'

'Like what?'

He wanted to tell her not to play dumb with him—but instead he made a sweeping movement with his hand intended to draw attention to the minute size of the accommodation as his mouth flattened into a disapproving line.

As an architect, he had been schooled in aesthetics—but for Xandros the love of beauty had always been instinctive, rather than taught. He knew that taste was a purely subjective matter—but his early life in Greece had made him appreciate space and simplicity. Whereas this...

The clutter of her home was unbelievable—and the early-morning light picked it out with cruel clarity. It wasn't just the baby stuff—it was all the candles and knick-knacks she had everywhere. Not only was every surface covered with something which to his eyes seemed completely unnecessary—but now there was a double buggy to contend with.

The last time he'd been here he had barely noticed the jostle for space—for he had only been interested in taking her to bed and then getting the hell out of there. But where she lived affected *his* children.

'It's a mess!' he snapped.

'Well, it's my mess!' she said defiantly.

'Not necessarily.'

Rebecca stared at him—wondering how she could be so tired when she'd only just got up. They had told her at the hospital that she would get weary, but somehow she had thought that she'd be able to overcome any rogue fatigue through a sheer sense of will and determination. And she had been wrong. She had just fed, bathed and changed her two adorable little black-haired babies and now felt as if she had been wrung out to dry and then rained on all over again.

But Xandros's words made her eyes narrow with suspicion—because she had come to recognise the menace which underpinned that particularly silky tone of his. Her fatigue suddenly receded into the background. 'What do you mean?' she questioned.

He paused to give his statement significance—as he had done at high-powered boardroom meetings all his life. 'Just that what you choose to do in your life is entirely up to you, *agape mou*—but when it involves my children, then I surely have some say in the matter? Some influence as to how I think they should be brought up. And where.'

Rebecca swallowed, suddenly nervous as her mind skittered over all the possible replies she might make—knowing that it had to be the *right* reply when she was dealing with a man like Xandros. If she objected on the grounds that they weren't together as a couple any more—mightn't he think she was hinting that she'd like them to be? And yet—did he really have any rights to lay down the law about the twins' upbringing? Soon he would be gone—back to America and the life he had there. A life which did not include her or the boys, and never would.

'Do you really think it's any of your business?' she questioned.

He felt the sudden stirring of battle-lines being drawn and the adrenalin began to course through his veins. He had expected to feel nothing but impartial interest towards these two children who had sprung from his loins. He had told himself that it was simply curiosity which had compelled him to fly to Britain to see them. But he had been wrong.

During the three nights when she had been with them in hospital his thoughts had run riot in a way which was uncharacteristic—but the one thought which had overridden every other was that he wanted some part of his sons' lives.

'I plan to make it my business,' he said.

Rebecca heard the unmistakable challenge in his voice and something inside her quailed because she didn't doubt him, not for a moment. Imagine all the resources a man like Xandros could summon up to support any claim he might wish to make. It would need a strong and very rich woman to fight him—and, while she was working on the strength bit, she couldn't just snap her fingers to put herself on an equal financial footing with the Greek billionaire.

Wouldn't it be better to try to accommodate his wishes, rather than engaging in some kind of battle which he would be bound to win? He lived in America, for heavens' sake! Contact with him would be minimal, if she played this carefully. *So do it.*

'What did you have in mind?' she asked cautiously.

He glared at the door which led through to the tiny kitchenette. 'Well, for a start—this place is much too small.'

Rebecca nodded, knowing she'd sound both stubborn and ignorant if she disagreed—because he was right. 'And?'

'And I want you to move somewhere bigger.'

She sighed. She wasn't stupid. It had taken her about three seconds of being home with the babies to realise that the place simply wouldn't do—no matter how much she had tried to justify it in her head beforehand. But even if she touched the money which Xandros had been paying into her account—generous as it was—it still wouldn't go anywhere near a decent deposit on a bigger home. 'It isn't as easy as that, Xandros. Property in London is astronomically expensive.'

'I can afford it.'

'Yes, I know you can.' She swallowed. 'And what if I said that I didn't want to accept your—'

'Charity?' he intercepted sarcastically, his black eyes glittering with growing impatience. 'But this isn't about charity—or your misplaced feelings of pride. In fact, this has nothing to do with *you*, Rebecca—but my desire to ensure that my children don't grow up with less space than your average battery hen has to contend with!'

She stared at him. 'How dare you say something as hurtful as that?'

He shrugged, uncaring of her rage, or her hurt. 'Because it's the truth. You know it is.' His mouth hardened with determination. 'Whereas I am offering you the opportunity to move somewhere more suitable. You can live anywhere you like in this city. Anywhere at all.'

Pride or no pride, Rebecca wouldn't have been human if she hadn't felt a shiver of real longing at what he was proposing. He was blazing into her life and offering to rescue them all—and how many people ever got this kind of Cinderella chance to move from scullery to palace in one leap? But at what price?

She lifted her head to meet his gaze full on. 'And what if I say no?'

His expression was hard and uncompromising. Would she really dare to try to oppose his wishes? Did she know what kind of an adversary she would be taking on? 'I wouldn't advise saying no,' he warned softly.

His stony black gaze bored into her and, for possibly the first time, Rebecca realised what she was up against. Yes, he was enormously rich and that kind of wealth could buy you untold power, but with Xandros it was something much more than wealth.

She saw the steely determination to get exactly what he wanted—fired by some primitive urge to fight for the very best for his children. And could she really condemn him for having their best interests at heart? Could she? Would two increasingly mobile and lively little boys thank her for turning down the offer of a lifetime, simply because their father didn't love her? Pride was a terrible reason for denying her sons what was rightfully theirs.

'If…if I did agree—you mean *I* can choose where to live?' she questioned uncertainly.

Xandros turned away to look out of the window— as if checking to see whether the rain had stopped, but in reality to hide his small smile of triumph, knowing that he had won.

'Of course you can choose,' he murmured.

CHAPTER EIGHT

'JUST what kind of house *do* you like, Rebecca?' Xandros demanded impatiently one morning as he stood in her sitting room, which felt like a sauna and looked like a laundry—there were so many Babygros steaming dry on the radiator. Who would have thought that at this time in his life he would find himself sleeping on a woman's sofa in such a confined space? Moodily, he stared at all the specifications she had been shown and which she had rejected. 'Anything specific?'

Rebecca forced herself to concentrate on house details, and not on the moody expression on his dark, rugged face. Choosing a place to live when there were no financial limitations actually made a decision harder, she had discovered. How much easier it would have been to have ruled out most of the market because it was non-affordable. Too much choice, she had come to realise, actually provided its own kind of headache. But anything would be better than having Xandros camped and cramped on her sofa—making her feel the kind of things she definitely knew she shouldn't be feeling.

'Well, I don't want to live in one of those bleak-looking penthouses which resemble some kind of laboratory, that's for sure.'

Xandros gave a short laugh, wondering what his award-winning colleague who'd designed it would think of her dismissive attitude. 'Perhaps you'd like to tell me what you consider important?' He forced himself to treat her as if she were one of his clients. 'If you were given an ideal home—what one thing would it have to make it special?'

That was easy. Well, if you discounted the fairy tale…what had she missed most since moving to the capital? 'A garden,' she said instantly. 'That's all.'

'That's all?' Xandros gave a wry smile. Ironically, what she wanted was more elusive than any award-winning development. Was she being disingenuous or just genuinely innocent of the market? 'Garden space in London is like gold-dust.' He nodded. 'But I know some people I can get onto it. Let me see to that.'

Rebecca pushed her fingers back through her untidy hair, resenting the way he could just snap his fingers and have a whole assortment of people to do all the running for him—but a feeling which was bigger than resentment was gnawing away at her.

Didn't he realise that all this wasn't easy? Going through all the motions of choosing a brand-new home, but without all the normal stuff that most new mothers might expect. Like the shared excitement of a couple in love. All she had was Xandros talking about putting *his people* onto it, in that cold and uncaring manner. Pretty much the same way that he'd dealt with everything else. 'Fantastic,' she said, with faint sarcasm.

His eyes narrowed—her attitude like a slap in the face to his macho Greek pride—and he felt the slow burn of anger, and something else too. Something which had been building inside him no matter how much he had tried to tell himself that it was no longer appropriate. 'Such a truculent approach, *agape*,' he murmured. 'I thought you might at least be a little grateful.'

'Did you?' How many more expectations of her would he have? She had let him name the babies and sleep on her sofa and now she was letting him change the very fabric of her life. Where the hell was this all going to end? Rebecca glanced over at him, steeling herself against the sight of him leaning against the window sill—black denim encasing the muscular thrust of his thighs and a dark cashmere sweater clinging lovingly to the hard lines of his torso.

His black hair was ruffled, the ebony eyes were glittering with life and vitality and there was the dark hint of shadow around the strong jaw. This was Xandros at his most casual and sexy—and, heaven help her, but she wanted him. Was it normal for a woman to feel the slow, heavy ache of desire when she'd only recently given birth? Or was that just because he was Xandros? Because she had loved him and tasted the pleasures of his body so many times that maybe he'd spoilt her for any other man.

Gazing at the soft, olive gleam of his skin and re-membering what it felt like to have it wrapped around her naked body, it was easy to forget all their turbu-lent history—even easier to forget that he was only here because he had to be. *He's only here because of the babies,* she reminded herself painfully. She told herself that it shouldn't hurt, but it did, of course it did—and she found herself wanting to hurt him back. To show him that she wasn't going to act like a starving puppy who was just grateful for any old scrap he happened to throw in her direction.

'And does my lack of gratitude rile you, Xandros? Would you like me to throw myself slavishly at your feet? Is that what you'd like?'

He heard the note of defiance in her voice and something like victory began to bubble in his veins. At last! It was the taunt he had wanted, the one which at some deep level of his subconscious he'd been praying for. The casting aside of the polite niceties. The green light to do what he most wanted to do.

Like some dark panther, he moved silently towards her, seeing her violet eyes darken and her rose-petal lips part. 'What do you think I'd like you to do, *agape*?'

She wasn't doing much in the way of thinking, not when standing so close that she could detect that lemony, masculine scent of his—and her senses had automatically begun to silently scream their appreciation and their hunger. Too late she saw the danger of his nearness and the spell it cast over her. And he wielded that danger like a weapon, she realised—he was perfectly aware of his own power. Yet crazily, she didn't resent it—for wasn't this the first indication that he still found her desirable? And wasn't that reassuring, even if it was inappropriate? 'X-Xandros?' she breathed. 'Wh-what is this all about?'

'Oh, Rebecca. Isn't it a waste of time to ask a

question to which you already know the answer?' he mocked as he pulled her, soft and unresisting, into his arms.

'Don't—'

'Don't what, *agape*? Don't do what your eyes are begging me to do, even if your mind isn't quite sure you should be letting me?'

His perception was almost as unsettling as his proximity. His warm breath stirred the tiny hairs on her neck as he whispered against it and Rebecca felt herself begin to shiver—hating the accuracy of his words and hating the sudden clamouring need of her body. His hands were holding her firmly by the waist and it seemed like a lifetime since he had touched her like this.

'Xandros—'

'What?'

'Stop it.'

'But you don't want me to. Do you?' The pad of his thumb began to trace a line over the silken surface of her neck and he felt her shiver beneath his touch. 'Mmm. You smell delicious and you feel delicious.'

'I smell of baby-milk.'

'I know you do. And that's delicious. You're delicious.'

Was she? Really? Rebecca felt her heart-rate soar. He murmured as if it did not bother him that her body was still thick after having given birth to his children. As if he didn't care that she hadn't washed her hair for two days. And his fingers were moving down to touch the softness of her belly with shocking intimacy, making her yearn to have him drift them downwards and bring her to such quick and effortless pleasure, as he had done so many times in the past. She could feel the honeyed rush of desire and the urgent acceleration of her heart. 'Xandros!' she breathed.

'Do you like that?'

She mocked him back with his own words. 'Isn't it a waste of time to ask a question to which you already know the answer?'

He laughed, but it was a laugh edged with anger and frustration and other stuff, too—stuff that he did not want to hold up for analysis. 'Then let's stop asking questions and let me kiss you instead.' Turning her face upwards, he stared down at her wide-eyed expression before he brought his lips down onto hers. She tasted of toothpaste and of coffee and she smelt of baby and he didn't think he had ever known a more unexpectedly powerful aphrodisiac. Because he had never tasted a woman in these circumstances before? Yes, that had to be it.

'Rebecca,' he groaned, against her lips. 'Oh, Rebecca.'

'Xandros,' she whispered back, as if they had just been introduced. Her arms clung to his broad shoulders like a tenacious vine and she could feel her body softening and responding—the ache inside her building by the instant.

It was the sweetest kiss she could ever remember— but maybe that was because it had been so long since he had kissed her. Or perhaps because the feminine side of her nature yearned for the perfect celebration to seal the birth of their children. She opened her lips to his and stifled a little moan as she lost herself in the sheer pleasure of it.

He held back as he grazed his mouth against hers as if he were discovering it through touch alone. 'I want to take you to bed,' he said unsteadily. 'But perhaps it is too soon.'

She knew that; she wanted it too. Yet this could not be right, could it? Not on so many levels which had nothing to do with the fact that she had only recently given birth. Warning bells rang loud in her head. Their relationship was over—and Xandros was in the process of calling the shots. Insisting that she move somewhere bigger, which *he* was going to pay for. And even though she knew that made sense, if she then allowed him to engage in easy sex—wouldn't that make her look morally corrupt? As if she were selling herself for favours?

Next thing and he'd be employing some hot-shot lawyer to insist that she was morally unfit to bring up his children. She wouldn't put it past him. Come to think of it—she wouldn't put anything past him.

More than that, she still had feelings for him—of course she did. Trying to fall out of love with somebody wasn't like turning off a light switch—it was more like an unpredictable sea and you still got waves of it washing over you when you least expected it. There was a pretty big one threatening to engulf her right now.

Even though her breasts were tingling and the heavy beat of blood had begun to throb shamefully at all her pulse points, Rebecca pushed at the hard wall of his chest, resisting the urge to creep her fingers beneath his shirt and trickle at the whorls of hair with her nails. How much of sexual reaction was habit and conditioning? she wondered hazily. Yet surely the ache in her heart had nothing to do with habit?

'We must stop this right now, Xandros,' she said. 'This is wrong! You know it is!'

Wrong? He had to fight every instinct he possessed to allow her to break the embrace, but Xandros let her pull fractionally away from him, his breathing ragged as he waited for the hard heat of desire to subside.

'No,' he negated harshly as he stared down into her darkened eyes—seeing the full flush of desire in her cheeks and the tremble of her lips. 'That is where you are so very mistaken, my beauty. Of all things in this whole crazy situation apart from our beautiful children—this…*this*…' and he arrogantly brushed his palm over her breasts, feeling them pin-point into life against him '…is the only thing which is remotely right between us.' Black eyes roved over her in critical assessment. 'And you are a hypocrite if you deny that to yourself, Rebecca—let alone to me.'

More than anything she wanted to reach up and pull his dark head down towards her and to continue losing herself in another sweet, drugging kiss. But a kiss could fool you. It could make you imagine stuff which wasn't there and Rebecca couldn't face any more hurt. Not now—when she had to be strong for her boys. Xandros didn't love her and there was nothing to be gained from thinking that he ever would.

Afraid to inflame him—or herself—any further, she took a step back, playing for time as she reminded herself of the reality, rather than fantasy. Because soon he would be gone from her life—back to his glitzy tower in New York—and the last thing she needed was to tie herself closer to him emotionally.

'Yes, the sex was always very good,' she agreed brutally. 'I'm sure it always is with you—but that that's not relevant any more, Xandros.'

'You don't think so?' he taunted silkily.

'I know so. When our relationship ended—it ended. We can't just pretend that didn't happen simply because we still happen to desire one another. It isn't fair on anyone.'

He stared into the violet-blue eyes, forcing his desire to subside as he registered that she meant it. And yet strangely he had never respected her quite as much as he did right then—with her untidy hair and her defiant expression and her bold statement. When had a woman last taken the facts and looked at them with cool assessment before standing her ground like that— against what they both really wanted and against his wishes?

'Very well. I will concentrate instead on what needs to be done. You want a garden, and you shall have a garden. I will make sure we have a house by the end of the week,' he vowed softly.

There was the tiniest of pauses. *We.* Rebecca was certain it was a slip of the tongue—it *had* to be. She gave him a nervous smile. 'And you'll be going back to the States soon, I expect. You have a business to run.'

Xandros heard the hope in her voice, even though he could see she was doing her best to disguise it. And in that moment, something inside him changed.

Up until now he had not thought beyond the next action—and that had been the need to get her and the babies out of this coop of a place. But Rebecca's words forced him to look further into a future where two little babies who carried half his genes would be growing up into boys, and then men. And then what? Didn't he need to stamp his presence on their conscious minds—to bond with them early so that they would know him as their father?

After all, who knew what their mother might do once she realised that he really was *not* planning to marry her? Who was to say that she wouldn't grow bored with the daily grind of child-rearing and long for some kind of excitement which would take her away from it—as his own mother had done. And who better to step in, if that should be the case?

But only if they know you.

He gave her a hard, glittering smile. 'I don't remember saying anything about going back to the States,' he said.

Something warned her as surely as if a cold, clammy hand had reached out and grabbed her by the back of the neck. 'But I thought—'

'What?' he enquired, mock-pleasantly. 'What did you think, Rebecca?'

Don't let him intimidate you—because if you show weakness, then you really will be lost.

'Well, your offices are in New York, aren't they? And you're a busy man—you certainly can't afford the time to hang around here.'

'Can't I?' His black eyes bored into her with something approaching amusement. What did she think he was going to do? Pay up for her to live in luxury and then creep away like some kind of patsy? 'I can do whatever I like, Rebecca—and what I'd like right now is to be close to my children. I want to be there when they wake up in the morning and turn the light out last thing at night.'

It took several seconds for his meaning to sink in, and when it did she felt almost light-headed with fear. 'You mean...you mean...you're planning to *move in* with us?'

He watched the colour drain from her face, saw the violet eyes cloud with apprehension, but he hardened his heart against the expression in them. 'Of course I am. How could you ever consider otherwise?' He leaned forward and his eyes were as cold as the black ice which glittered on the roads during the most unforgiving of winter days. 'Did you really think that I was going to buy you a big house and then be airbrushed from my sons' lives? Did you really think I was the type of man to pay all the bills and then be sidelined, Rebecca? I'm not quite of the right age to be considered for the role of sugar-daddy.'

She opened her mouth to tell him that *he* had been the one to insist on a bigger place to live—and now he was holding her to ransom over it. Twisting it round to make her sound like some manipulative gold-digger just out for what she could get! Was he so rich that he hadn't bothered to check that she hadn't touched a penny of the money he had been sending her? 'And what if I told you that I would rather stay in this cramped place than share a palace with you?'

His smile was grim, but the fire of battle was heating his blood. 'Then you would be opening the floodgates for me to mount a legal challenge for custody of the boys.'

'You wouldn't!'

'Oh, I would, Rebecca—believe me, I would.'

'You won't get it!' she breathed. 'You know you won't!'

'Maybe not sole custody,' he conceded, 'since the courts still tend to favour the mother. But there is no reason why I shouldn't be awarded joint custody. And how would you feel then, Rebecca—if I started taking Andreas and Alexius to New York every other week?'

To her horror, she saw a new light appear in his black eyes—as if this was an option he hadn't previously considered, one which she had illuminated by challenging him. And he could do it, she recognised painfully. He could forge a life with the twins which might gradually exclude her—because what little boy wouldn't leap to have the kind of father who could provide the kind of upbringing that Xandros could? What could she offer which could compare?

Fiercely, she dug her fingernails into the palms of her hands. She could offer them something which they could never get from anyone else—a mother's love!

Her mind was spinning. She had managed to back herself into a corner—she knew it, and she was pretty sure that he knew it, too. *So act calm. Don't let him know how frightened you are. Put on a brave face and stand up to him—if not for your sake, then for the sake of your boys.*

'Very well,' she said slowly. 'If moving in with us is your condition for providing our sons with the space and the comfort they deserve—then so be it.' She drew in a deep breath. 'But I think you had better hear mine, Xandros.'

'*Ne*, I am fascinated to hear what that will be, *agape*,' he mocked, tilting his dark head to one side. 'Or shall I guess? Mmm? Are you going to say that you don't want me to kiss you as I did just now? Or to touch you or to bring you any number of the countless pleasures we both know could be yours in an instant? Am I right, Rebecca? Yes, I can see that I am—for your face flames just as I have seen it flame so many times when you have cried out in my arms.'

Despite the sensual provocation of his words, Rebecca forced herself not to react to them. 'That's right,' she said calmly. 'If we live under the same roof, then it must be separately.'

'Separately,' he echoed thoughtfully, but his smile was that of the unashamed predator. Did she really think that would satisfy a man of his sexual appetite? And what about her own, come to that? Hadn't she just demonstrated how much she still wanted him? 'We'll see how long you are content to live like that, *agape mou*,' he finished softly.

CHAPTER NINE

XANDROS bought a house in Holland Park—an up-market area of London which Rebecca had only ever passed through on a bus. It was a large four-storey building in a deceptively quiet tree-lined road—with plenty of young families living around.

The sort of house you could easily fall in love with, thought Rebecca wistfully. *His* house, she reminded herself as they each carried a baby into the oak-lined hallway, where stained glass from the front door spilled bright colours onto the black and white tiled floor.

Within hours of their arriving, a glamorous blonde neighbour named Caroline had arrived, bearing an expensive bottle of champagne, a plate of smoked-salmon sandwiches and an invitation to a drinks party she was having.

'You will come, won't you?' she asked Rebecca, but her eyes and her smile kept flicking to the tall and silent Greek who was leaning on the door-jamb.

Rebecca didn't really know how to reply. She was aware of Xandros's dark, brooding face—probably keen to establish that, although they might *look* like a conventional family, they were anything but. And maybe socialising with the neighbours would require too much in the way of acting skills.

'We'll see how we're fixed,' said Rebecca diplomatically, recognising that an outright refusal might lead to pressure from their attractive new neighbour— if the determined light in her eyes was anything to go by.

But the house itself was out of this world. It was the kind of place she could never have imagined living in—with its tall, spacious rooms and its sweeping staircase—yet her transition from poky little apartment to turn-of-the-century splendour had been frighteningly effortless.

Xandros had overseen everything—arranging for a designer to fill the house with carefully chosen pieces of furniture, and exquisite drapes to be hung at the floor-to-ceiling windows. There was a wonderful nursery for Alexius and Andreas—with her own bedroom and bathroom next door.

Xandros had put in a whole suite for himself on the top floor—including a big, airy studio with fabulous views overlooking the park. From there he could work, he told her—since these days an architect could work from anywhere. It made her wonder what his plans were—and just how long-term the arrangement was supposed to be.

But the time for asking was not now and she doubted he would tell her even if she did. And what was the point in worrying over something which she couldn't control? She was too busy counting her blessings and realising just how cramped it had been at her little apartment—and how unfair it would have been on the twins to allow that state to continue. Here was the space she had been promised and for the time being it eclipsed all the potential problems of sharing a house with a man as dangerously attractive as Xandros.

She felt her spirits lighten as she stared out at her beautiful new garden, with its curved flower-beds and tall trees—imagining two rapidly growing little boys toddling around in it. She would make them a sandpit, she decided. And get them a little plastic slide. She thought of them asleep and fed upstairs in their cream and azure haven of a bedroom and she gave a secret smile of pleasure.

Xandros was watching her—registering the slow curving of her lips, which reminded him why her particular beauty had first so transfixed him, along with those blue-violet eyes and hair like molten honey. How long since he had buried his mouth in that hair? How long since he had kissed those lips? He felt the impatient stir of frustration. If he walked up to her and took her into his arms, he had not a single doubt that he could have her responding to him in an instant.

Yet for the moment something stopped him and maybe it was the strange new air of composure and serenity which had settled on her, like a mantle. He had noticed it earlier—when she had been sitting in a chair by the window in the nursery, feeding Alexius, his twin brother asleep in a Moses basket by her feet. Like a subtle spotlight, the pale sunlight had illuminated them and given the scene an unexpected radiance—

turning the honey of her hair into spun-gold. And in that moment, she had never looked more beautiful.

Was that yet another example of the random lottery of life? he wondered abstractedly. That some women should take to motherhood as if they had been born for it—while others...

'Rebecca?'

Rebecca turned around from the window, bracing herself against his physical impact, because no matter how many times she looked at him she could do nothing to stop herself from melting.

He was sitting on one of the two sofas—his long legs spread out in front of him in unconsciously elegant pose, beautifully cut dark trousers encasing muscular thighs, and she had to swallow against the sudden dryness in her throat.

'Yes, Xandros?'

She was back to wearing jeans, he noticed. Without any fuss or discussion or unattractive, sweat-filled trips to the gym, she seemed to have regained those amazing, lush curves with all the healthy vigour of youth and vitality. He wanted to slide them off and thrust into her, and... He swallowed. Damn her, and damn her beauty! 'We need to discuss arrangements,' he said huskily.

'What kind of arrangements?' she questioned.

'About hiring a nanny,' he drawled. 'Unless you'd prefer to discuss alternative sleeping arrangements? I know I would.'

She drew a deep breath—trying to ignore the sensual invitation in his words, the way his black eyes were insolently travelling over her body, as if they had every right to do so. She had heard the expression 'undressing you with his eyes' but she had never really known what it meant until she had met Xandros.

But the undeniable sexual tension which simmered under the surface was now only one facet of a life which had suddenly become full. Motherhood was a job, she had realised—and, more than that, it was one she could do well, which brought her confidence, and a quiet self-assurance. The Rebecca who had so vainly spent her time trying to appease the exacting Xandros had gone.

'I don't want to hire a nanny,' she said quietly.

Xandros frowned—because this wasn't what he had expected either. Hadn't he thought that once she recognised he wasn't going anywhere there would be demands for all kinds of trappings? Wealth bought hired help—and some women liked that. 'Do you have any idea of the work involved once they start getting older? Of the way it's going to restrict your freedom?'

'Of course I do! Everything just takes twice as long, that's all. But you would know that better than anyone.' She sat down on the window-seat. 'Xandros—you could actually give me a little insight here—how did *your* mother manage?'

There was a pause. Normally he would have automatically deflected her question and, in the circumstances, perhaps he could acknowledge its relevance—but that didn't mean he liked her asking. 'I don't think she'd be a particularly good role model for new mothers of twins,' he said coolly.

'Why not?'

Xandros met her steady gaze with an instinctive flash of irritation because he hated digging beneath the surface of facts. Once, she would have correctly interpreted his mood and immediately stopped her line of questioning. Back then she would have done anything he wanted her to do. But now he could see that she'd changed—of course she had. Going through a pregnancy on your own and then giving birth to two babies and not knowing how the hell you were going to support them would be bound to change a woman.

Did that give her the right to know more about his history? And was his reluctance to tell her less about a fierce desire for privacy and more to do with the fact that he had buried it so deep, for so many years, that he had no desire to resurrect it?

'Because my mother left when Kyros and I were very young.'

She stared at him, her heart beating very fast. 'She *left*?'

'But fathers leave all the time—and sometimes mothers, too.' He gave a mocking smile to disguise the faint pain which this old scar could still produce. And his surprise that it should. 'Surely that's true equality, Rebecca?'

'But...how old were you?'

'Four.' He shot the one word out repressively— along with an impatient glance. 'Look, she left us with my father, who was perfectly able to make sure that we were cared for. Kyros and I grew up fine—and that's it. No big drama.'

So how come his words had a hollow ring about them? 'It must have been difficult for your father to manage, though—with two little boys to care for,' she said slowly. 'How did he do it?'

'We had lots of different nannies who looked after us,' he said, and shrugged. 'My father was a busy man—driven by ambition and the will to succeed. His business demanded all the hours in the day. That's one of the things which drove my mother into the arms of another man, or so she claimed. She wanted excitement and glamour—and an absentee husband and two demanding children just didn't do it for her.'

'And you never see her?'

'No.' Now his eyes were like flint. 'She's dead. She died a few years after she left. We saw her only twice after she'd gone.' He remembered the man she had gone on to marry, the man who had replaced his father. Remembered wanting to punch him.

Rebecca nodded. In a way, the answers only threw up yet more questions. She wanted to ask them—of course she did—but the last thing Xandros would welcome were any clumsy attempts to be an amateur psychologist. There was a difference between being curious and prying. And something in his face told Rebecca not to push it.

Yet she recognised that for a man like Xandros whose emotions were clam-tight—this was a revelation indeed. It began to make his behaviour more understandable—that she had been guilty of thinking of him as a *type*, rather than a man. Cynicism didn't just spring from nowhere, she realized. It didn't matter how rich or powerful you were, there was always a reason for the person you became. Growing up with no mother as a role model said volumes about his take-it-or-leave-it attitude to women and his reluctance to be pinned down.

But the brief light he had shone into his past, and what it revealed, had unsettled her. Despite his assertion that it was no big deal and despite the flinty expression on that hard and beautiful face, she felt her heart ache for the deserted little boy he must have been. And surely he and his brother should be *close* now, instead of estranged? Especially after all they had gone through as children.

Once, she had been prepared to tiptoe around his feelings, but not any more. She wanted to go beyond all that pretence and subterfuge. Not for *her* sake—because she recognised that whatever they'd had between them had died—but for the sake of their two children. Yet she recognised too that confidences couldn't be rushed. He had to learn to trust her first—and maybe he never would.

And didn't she have to start being mature about circumstances herself? Didn't the sense of liberation that this beautiful house gave her fill her with relief? Was it her imagination, or had Alexius and Andreas settled to sleep far more easily than usual since they'd moved in—their mood been sunnier?

'I want to thank you,' she said awkwardly.

His eyes narrowed. 'For?'

'For making all this possible. For giving my sons all this space.'

'They're my *sons*, too,' he said bitterly. 'What the hell did you think I would do, Rebecca? Stand back while you brought them up in poverty?'

She wasn't going to argue that his definition of poverty wasn't the same as most people's. 'I didn't really give it much thought—how could I have done?

I didn't plan it.' She paused, waiting for the question which didn't come, but seeing it unmistakably written in his black eyes. 'No, I didn't,' she said fervently. 'But it's happened and I want to make the best of it. I want to be the best mother I possibly can—and for me that means being hands-on. I don't want a nanny.'

'It's too much for you to take on,' he said roughly.

Was he basing his response on the fact that his mother hadn't been able to cope? But no two women were the same. She shook her head, drawing a deep breath. 'Let me finish. I'm aware that in many ways I'm very lucky that you can afford to *offer* me a nanny—but I don't want some other woman impacting on the way my children are brought up.'

'You can't manage on your own in a house this size,' he persisted stubbornly.

'You're right, I can't.' She gave him a tentative smile, wishing that she could reach out and touch his face—not in a sexual way, but to ease some of the pain she read etched on his hard, stony features. 'You've seen what I'm like with clutter—so maybe the money would be better spent employing some kind of cleaner or housekeeper, who could keep the place up to your own exacting standards.'

She made him sound like some kind of robot, living in a sterile environment! And yet, her teasing tone made him give a wry smile as he realised that somehow—impossibly—she had got her own way. And it hadn't even felt like a battle. His smile vanished to be replaced by a thoughtful frown. Was Rebecca simply playing a clever game to reject his offer of a nanny? he wondered.

Was she aware that babies became little more than cute accessories in the world he inhabited? Dressed up in mini versions of the latest fashionable clothes worn by their oh-so-chic mamas. Brought out at parties, or occasionally whisked by at a lunch party to be cooed over and then handed back to some pasty-faced girl who would one day be disregarded and erased from that child's life. Maybe she thought that the novel would appeal to him—a woman who was actually willing to get her hands dirty.

Or maybe she wanted the boys to become so attached to her that they would be reluctant to have her leave them. Wouldn't that effectively stymie any attempts to get them to settle with him on the other side of the Atlantic?

Xandros gave a short laugh. What a cynical bastard he had become. 'Okay, Rebecca,' he said slowly. 'Let's get a housekeeper.'

CHAPTER TEN

THE morning sun bathed the desk with a crimson glow and Xandros put his pencil down, and stretched his arms above his head. He had been working since first light in his big, bare studio and had discovered that he could be extraordinarily productive in the quiet of this early-morning house.

He sat back, pleased with the first-stage drawing of the Parisian concert hall he was designing—which was scheduled to stand on the Left Bank, a new monument for one of the most beautiful cities in the world. His talent for design meant that he had always earned commissions from all over the world—and, of course, this base in London made a perfect base for travelling in Europe. No time-lag, either.

It was funny, really. You never knew how something would actually work out—no matter how carefully you planned it. It was like designing a building. The drawings could be perfect, the construction done exactly as you would wish it to be—yet it was usually the unpredictable which gave the place its character. When you were planning a structure—like the huge

research centre he had recently completed in Denver—
you could have no idea that the way the midday sun
hit its many faceted windows at noon would cause it
to be for ever known as The Diamond.

It was a bit like that here—living with Rebecca and
his sons. For all that the nature of his work made him
see bricks and mortar grow into something beautiful,
he had never realised that it could be like that with
children, too. That their daily development could be
as amazing as one of the tall buildings he'd conceived,
which seemed to defy gravity itself. But then, maybe
he'd never stopped to think about it before. Why would
he? There had never been any plans for him to become
a father until the situation had been forced on him.

But now his days had taken on their own routine—
of him leaving his work at lunchtimes and taking a
walk with Rebecca and the boys. His colleagues back
in the States would have been nonplussed to have seen
him taking an hour out of the day to stroll around a
park with a buggy. Come to think of it—he was pretty
baffled by it himself.

The faint sound of a whimper on the floor below
meant that one of the babies was waking, and the other
would soon follow—and he would go downstairs and
make a pot of coffee before the housekeeper arrived.
And then he would go and find Rebecca, who would
be doing something with one of the babies, wearing an
old pair of jeans, with her long hair tied back in a
ribbon, looking more beautiful than any woman had a
right to look.

But the image they presented to the outside world
of a happy couple had no real substance. It was like

one of those *trompe-l'oeil* paintings which tricked the eye into believing that you were looking at a real landscape—when really it was just a clever, two-dimensional painting.

He made coffee, picked up a couple of voice mail messages and went to find her in the nursery, where she was just towelling dry one of the babies. The damp from the bath was making her shirt cling to her breasts. Her beautiful breasts. 'There's been another message from that woman,' he said unevenly.

Rebecca looked up from the baby, thinking how perfect both boys were with their faintly olive-sheened skin so like their father, and the same jet-black hair and matching eyes. So far she could see nothing of herself in either of them. She frowned. 'Which woman?'

'The blonde, from next door. The one with the skirts—or, rather, the one *without* the skirts.'

Rebecca sat back on her heels, telling herself not to react. *Ah, yes. That one.* She looked down to straighten a corner of the little mat the baby was lying on. Of *course* Xandros would have noticed the rather inappropriate outfits and long legs of their neighbour and he was free to spend as much time as he liked studying them. The fact that she didn't like it was neither here nor there. She had elected for separate lives, and that was what she had got. *Be careful what you wish for.* 'What does she want this time?'

'She says she's left several messages. It's her drinks party tomorrow night and she wants us to go.'

Rebecca grimaced. 'You go. I'll stay here.'

Xandros watched as she deftly put the baby into his little blue suit. Wasn't it crazy how things changed?

He remembered the way he used to telephone her at the last moment to ask her for dinner and she used to drop everything to meet him. The way she used to fit in with his plans, and act as if she didn't care if he cancelled at the last minute. And hadn't he looked down on her for it? The way he had scorned all women who made it too easy for him.

But Rebecca certainly wasn't making it easy for him—not any more—and somewhere along the way he had stopped thinking it might be some clever game she was playing. No, this seemed to be deadly serious. When she had first told him she wanted separate rooms he had assumed that she was just going through the motions. Of maybe punishing him before welcoming him back into her arms and her bed. For how could she resist him, when no woman ever had?

He had even allowed himself to savour the anticipation of the inevitable, because he knew she still wanted him. He could easily read the tell-tale signs of desire, even though she tried her best to hide them from him. But some signals were unconscious. A woman had no control over the instinctive darkening of her eyes when a man she wanted walked into a room. Or the faint parting of her lips as if she wanted him to kiss them.

Yet her manner towards him was rather how he imagined a young but determinedly strict teacher might be. Her attitude polite, but distant. When they were interacting with the twins she was sweet and helpful—why, he had even found himself helping out at bath-time! But somewhere along the way she had erected a kind of invisible barrier around herself—

and something was stopping him from attempting to dismantle it.

Was she deliberately capitalising on her untouchable Madonna image? he wondered. And did she know that she was driving him crazy? That he lay awake at night, racked with painful desire at the thought that on the floor below she was downstairs in a bed much too big for her? Maybe it was giving her some kind of pleasure to imagine his frustration. And maybe it was about time he did something about it…

'You go,' Rebecca repeated, breaking into his uncomfortably erotic thoughts.

He went over to stand beside her. Her hair was tied up in a high pony-tail, leaving her neck bare, and he found himself wanting to run his lips along it. 'She wants both of us to go,' he said huskily.

'Somehow, I doubt that. And even if it were the case—I don't suppose she'll be heartbroken if you turned up on your own.'

'And what's that supposed to mean?'

She wished he wouldn't stand so close. From here the hard, denim-clad leg was directly in her line of vision. She glanced up at him and that was even worse. Now she could see the full, hard, impressive length of his body. The jut of his hips, which was so arrogantly and fundamentally masculine. 'Oh, come on, Xandros—you know perfectly well what it means!' She pushed a strand of hair behind her ear. 'You can't be blind to the fact that the woman finds you attractive.'

He realised that her matter-of-fact manner was having a dangerous effect on his blood pressure.

Maybe if she'd behaved in a way which was jealous, or clingy—then he might have enjoyed escaping into the house next door. But somehow the very prospect of going there without her seemed lacklustre.

'Well, I think you should come as well,' he said silkily. 'In fact, I insist on it. It'll do you good. You haven't had a night out in—how long is it?'

Not since the early days of her pregnancy, but Rebecca was too proud to tell him that—especially in the light of that rather patronizing, 'It'll do you good.' 'Oh, not for ages,' she said vaguely. 'But that's quite common for new mothers.'

'Suddenly, you are the world expert on new mothers, are you?' he put in sardonically. 'Well, I want you to come. Look on it as a public relations exercise for the sake of our children—so that we can meet other parents in the street.'

'How very provincial that sounds,' she murmured.

He laughed softly. 'Are you accusing me of being provincial, *agape mou*? That is outrageous.'

This felt dangerously like flirting and Rebecca rose to her feet and nervously took a step back, like someone who had strayed just a little too close to the cliff-edge for comfort. 'Anyway, we don't have a baby-sitter.'

'Betty says she's happy to do it.'

Rebecca liked and trusted their housekeeper—and she'd been a mother herself and adored the twins. And it *had* been a long time since she'd gone out—especially to a party.

'Oh, okay,' she said. 'I'll come.'

Something she had been indifferent to suddenly

became something she began to get excited about—as Rebecca found herself looking forward to the party. Forgotten excitement began to bubble away inside her as she began to get ready. Maybe that was because she felt good about herself, she told herself. Because her self-esteem was in place and she hadn't allowed herself to be bowled over like an emotional or physical ninepin.

But she still needed to be vigilant around Xandros. She had thought that, by maintaining her distance, her desire for him would lessen—but nothing could be further from the truth. She wanted him very badly and *knew* that he wanted her—yet something had changed.

She had his children now—they had forged two brand-new lives together and the emotional significance of that was deeply profound. They needed to maintain a civilised relationship for the future—no matter what that future was. And Xandros had all the weaponry in his armoury to hurt her in ways she couldn't even bear to imagine—and she couldn't allow that to happen. Not now. She couldn't afford to go to pieces with two beautiful little babies who relied on her. *So remember that next time he tempts you.*

On the night of the party, Betty took over. As a housekeeper she was superb—as a stand-in for the night, she was unmatchable. A kind but no-nonsense woman in her fifties, with her own grown-up children, she told Rebecca to go off and enjoy herself, and not to worry.

'For heaven's sake,' she said firmly. 'You're only next door if I need you!'

Spring was in the air and Rebecca chose a favourite pre-pregnancy outfit—one of those dresses which always made her feel wonderful and which she was delighted still fitted her. In filmy shades of blue, it fell softly to her ankles—thankfully concealing her winter-pale legs—and she teamed it with a beautiful pair of blue-jewelled sandals she'd bought in Rome, which added just the right, casual touch. Her hair she left loose and newly washed and she sprayed on a scent which smelt of roses.

Xandros was waiting for her in the drawing room, standing silhouetted against the vast window, and he turned round at the sound of her footsteps, his black eyes narrowing as he saw her. Her silken hair cascaded down around her shoulders, with two little clips keeping the mass of it from her face, and her blue-violet eyes were dark and wide. He felt the sudden hard beat of desire.

'You look beautiful,' he said softly.

'Don't sound so surprised.'

'Maybe I am. It's a long time since I've seen you dressed like that.'

'It's a long time since I've been out to a party.'

But her casual words masked what she was really feeling. That this felt uncomfortably like a date. It felt like something a *couple* would do. And they weren't a couple. They weren't. The last time she had dressed up like this had been that fateful night at her flat—when he had been so critical about where she lived and the effort she had made. *Remember* that *if you get carried away with the way his black eyes are caressing you now,* she told herself—*as if he would like to drag you off somewhere and* ravish *you.*

'I'd better check on the twins,' she said unsteadily.

'Rebecca, I've just checked—and they are fine. So is Betty. Now relax.'

Relax? That would be walking straight into the danger zone, surely? Relaxing meant letting her guard slip—and wouldn't that lead on to her looking at Xandros and deciding that he was irresistible, dressed in that dark shirt and trousers—with his ebony hair and eyes gleaming like jet?

She went to pick up the pale cashmere wrap but he took it from her.

'Here. Let me,' he said, and draped it carefully around her bare shoulders.

Rebecca felt herself trembling and wondered if he had noticed. Xandros was a maestro when it came to women. Did he realise how disturbing such a simple gesture could be—especially when you had been starved of physical contact for so long that your body was aching for it? And now? Was he deliberately brushing his fingers against her collar-bone, making her shockingly aware of how close they were to her breasts and how easy it would be for him to begin to stroke her there? And didn't she want that? Didn't she want to tremble with passion and desire again?

But it's over. It has to be over.

A rush of blood to her cheeks was only adding to her discomfort and she moved away from him, trying to subdue the aching in her body. 'Let's go,' she said unsteadily.

'Yes, let's,' he echoed, a faint smile playing at the corners of his mouth—like a man playing poker who realised he held the trump card.

The lighted window of the large house next door showed a party in full flow—with tiny women looking like exotic birds of paradise in their fine frocks and jewels, and men in dark suits standing in small clusters.

Caroline herself opened the door—almost, thought Rebecca, as if she'd been waiting for them. Had she? Or was that just her being paranoid? And even if she had been—it was none of Rebecca's business. She couldn't decide that she didn't want Xandros for herself—but then object if somebody else obviously did. Even if Caroline *was* a married woman, it was not her place to act as someone else's moral conscience.

Married or not, the way the blonde stuck to his side made it clear she had decided that Xandros was her number one favourite guest. And, in a way, Rebecca couldn't blame her. Hadn't she once been like that herself? Just one in a long line of docile women who were enraptured with the stunning Greek billionaire.

His exotic and rugged good looks made him stand out from the crowd of other men and he dominated the room as if he were lit by some dark, inner fire. He drew the eye like a magnet. Rebecca saw people edging closer, men *and* women, but especially women—trying to hear what he was saying, as if some force beyond their control were compelling them to do so.

'He's lovely,' said a woman who was standing close by and had been watching him.

'Yes,' said Rebecca.

'I believe you're the mother of his children?'

'That's right.'

'But you're not married?'

Rebecca turned to look at the other woman properly. Her eyes were bright with curiosity, her over-dieted face momentarily hard. Did she care that her unsubtle line of questioning might be hurtful? Of course she didn't. 'You seem to know an awful lot about me,' she commented wryly.

'I'm Caroline's sister. She's spoken of you. Said there's a new couple who'd moved in next door.' The woman forced a smile which did not meet the bright eyes, as if trying to establish a fact once and for all. 'But you're not his wife, right?'

'That's right,' said Rebecca—wondering whether it would have made any difference if she had been. Maybe these kind of women considered any man fair game, if the man happened to be alluring enough. She sipped her champagne, hoping it might dissolve some of the small knot of anguish inside her.

But in a way, Caroline's sister helped reinforce her conviction that she was doing the best thing by keeping her physical and emotional distance from Xandros. Why, if they were still lovers she would probably be spitting at the sight of their neighbour who was smiling into his eyes as if she was already imagining him in her bed. And where the hell *was* her poor husband?

She drank a glass of champagne and nibbled on a couple of carrot sticks, forcing herself to chat with some of the other guests. Just because she was all mixed-up about Xandros, didn't mean she couldn't be a good person to have at a party. She met another mother who lived on the other side of the park who was actually very sweet, and they arranged to meet for coffee.

She was just chatting to a rather dashing pianist from Uruguay with the darkest eyebrows she had ever seen, when there was a tap on her shoulder and she turned to find Xandros standing there with an impatient look on his face.

'Are you ready to go?' he asked.

She had actually been enjoying a grown-up conversation about classical music, and felt like telling him that she wanted to stay and learn a bit more. But they had been away for two hours, and she was keen to get back to the twins.

'I guess so.' She smiled at the pianist. 'I've so enjoyed talking to you,' she said.

He gave a rueful smile. 'Me, too,' he murmured. 'It's a pity you have to leave—and so early, too.'

Outside, the air was cool and they had just walked through their front gate when Xandros caught hold of her elbow, startling her as much with the unexpected contact as the undisguised hostility which was glittering from his black eyes.

'You know they say that he even flirts with the leg of his piano!' he accused, his hard, rugged features illuminated by the security lights which had caught them in their spotlight.

'Who does?' she asked, genuinely confused.

'Rodriguez. The man you couldn't take your eyes off!'

'It *is* usual to look at someone when they're speaking to you, Xandros!'

'Is it, *agape mou*?' he said softly. 'So why do you shy away when you're looking at *me*?'

'I don't.'

'Liar,' he taunted. 'Yes, you do. And do you know why?'

'N-no.' Suddenly, her hard-fought-for composure seemed to be slipping away—vanquished by the powerful aphrodisiac of his touch.

'Because if you allow yourself to look at me for long enough you will remember how it felt to have my lips on yours. My mouth on your body. You will think back to how it was to lie naked in my arms, your body sated and satisfied,' he finished, on a soft boast.

But not her heart, she realised—he had always left that empty and hungry for more. 'Xandros—'

'And you will realise that you are sick of living with memories. That you want that. Admit it, Rebecca—admit you still want me!'

'Xandros—' She said his name again and this time the word was supposed to be a protest—a soft indication that maybe they should stop all this. But perhaps it lacked conviction, for now his hand was cupping the other elbow and he was drawing her towards him as if she had been composed of nothing more substantial than a ball of cotton wool.

And she was letting him. He was moving her as if she were a puppet and he her master, but suddenly she didn't care. How could she care about anything when her senses were fizzing over like shaken-up champagne from which the cork had just been eased?

It had been so long since she had been in his arms like this. Not like that time at her flat, when she'd only recently given birth and she had been feeling awkward and unsure. Tonight, in her party dress and high heels—all perfumed and pampered—she felt like a real woman. And, oh, there was no doubt about the authenticity of this ultimate alpha-male who was now pulling her closer still.

She could feel the muscular strength of his powerful body and sense the rapid building of his desire as he tipped her face up to look at him. 'Did you want him?' he demanded roughly. 'Did you?'

'No—' But the word was lost as he crushed his mouth down on hers in a kiss which felt more about punishment than desire, and although Rebecca knew that she should not be responding to it—she just couldn't stop herself.

He was hot and aroused, his hands tumbling in her hair as if he had never touched her hair before, and his thigh was nudging insistently at hers, causing them to part and him to groan. 'Rebecca—'

Her hands flew up as she kissed him back with a fervour of someone who had never been kissed before, winding her arms sinuously around his neck, unable to get enough of him. She pressed herself into his body, but not as close as she wanted to be and she began to melt with unbearable longing. Why shouldn't she want him? When had she ever really stopped wanting him? She moaned softly as he splayed his hands over her buttocks and it made her long for him to touch the aching skin beneath. After all, they were two adults who were…were…'

'Miss Gibbs!'

A voice broke into her stupefied arousal and in a

daze Rebecca lifted her head as Xandros abruptly stopped kissing her—to see Betty standing at the top of the stairs leading to their front door, her face creased with concern.

'Miss Gibbs—can you come in? It's the baby. He's sick!'

CHAPTER ELEVEN

THEY heard the sound of a dreadful cough, which sounded like the barking of a seal, before they had even set foot inside the house.

'Which baby is it?' asked Rebecca desperately. As if it mattered!

'Alexius, I think!' answered Betty.

Rebecca moaned. No one knew them as she and Xandros knew them—so how could they have gone out when they were still so young? 'What happened?'

'He started coughing like that about half an hour ago and it's been getting worse. I think it's croup—my own had it.'

Croup? A vague memory of some respiratory condition swam into Rebecca's mind. Did she have it referenced in a book somewhere?

Xandros ran up the sweeping staircase with the two women following after him and Rebecca's terrible guilt was only increased as she ran into the nursery to see him cradling one of his sons who was making a horrible, wheezing sound.

'It's Alexius,' he said. His black eyes icy-bleak as they met hers.

Rebecca bit her lip. 'I'm going to ring the doctor,' she said, and turned to Betty. 'And then I want you to tell me exactly what you noticed.'

The doctor came quickly—a surprisingly young medic who barely looked old enough to have qualified, but he examined the baby with confident, gentle hands before straightening up.

'Your housekeeper's right. It's croup,' he said. 'Good old-fashioned croup.'

'Croup? What the hell is croup?' demanded Xandros.

'Inflammation of the upper airway,' said the medic. 'Not an uncommon condition for a young baby at this time of the year. You say he has a twin? I'd better take a look at him, too.'

'And the treatment?' Rebecca's voice was trembling. 'Will he have to be admitted to hospital?'

'That shouldn't be necessary, Miss Gibbs.' The doctor smiled. 'I'm afraid the treatment is rather old-fashioned, too—you need to sit up with him and keep him in a moist atmosphere. A steamy bathroom is perfect—you can both take it in turns to run the bath.'

Xandros stared at the doctor. 'You are telling me that, in this day and age, the only treatment is for us to *run the bath*?' he repeated incredulously.

'Just *do* it, will you, Xandros?' Rebecca pleaded.

He nodded, hearing the sudden steel which underpinned her plea. *'Ne, agape mou,'* he said softly. 'I will do it now.'

The doctor pronounced Andreas clear and told Rebecca to keep the two babies apart for a couple of days. 'I'll drop in first thing tomorrow morning,' he promised. 'And in the meantime—you've got a long night ahead of you both.'

Rebecca carried her son into the bathroom, which was now so steamy that it took a second or two for her eyes to become accustomed to the mist when suddenly Xandros's tall, shadowy figure appeared beside her and she started. But she had never been so glad to see someone in her life.

'Here, let me take him,' he said.

'In a minute.' Rebecca winced as her little baby began to wheeze. 'I want to hold him. Oh, Xandros, we shouldn't have gone to the party.'

'For heaven's sake!' he gritted. 'He was fine when we left—you know that, otherwise you would have refused to have gone. Do not blame yourself, Rebecca—for I will not let you. You are a good mother to our children,' he declared fiercely.

'None of it matters,' she whispered, perilously close to tears and yet knowing that she couldn't give in to them. 'The only thing that matters is that he gets better.'

'And he *will* get better.'

'Will he?' said Rebecca as she heard the fast, difficult breaths issuing from the little lungs and it felt as if someone were twisting a knife inside her.

'Of course he will,' said Xandros, with a conviction he did not feel—for this was something completely outside his domain and beyond his control. But his statement was intended to comfort Rebecca, not simply to ease his own, troubled thoughts.

How much happier he would have felt if the doctor had been able to give his son a tablet, or an injection—instead of this bizarre situation where he and Rebecca had to take it in turns to hold their coughing baby and keep renewing the hot water so that steam wafted in great warm clouds around them.

Their senses seemed disorientated by the misty atmosphere and the presence of fear. Never had seconds passed more slowly, nor minutes either. But eventually five became ten and then sixty and at last that first, difficult hour had gone. And with each passing hour, their son seemed less fretful than before. From being almost scared to breathe herself—for fear that she would miss any change in Alexius—Rebecca felt a little of the tension leave her body.

Was it her imagination, or did the child's breathing become easier as the first faint flush of dawn began to streak the sky outside?

'And to think I once thought that life in Greece was primitive,' Xandros murmured as the baby's wheezing gave way to the steadier tones of sleep and they looked at one another and instinctively knew that the danger had passed. 'Steam,' he said faintly, and shook his dark head with a wry smile.

'Oh, Xandros,' said Rebecca, and to her horror she began to cry, unable to stop the tears which were dripping down onto Alexius's head, but Xandros wiped them away with his fingertips as fast as they fell.

'Sshh.' Shaken, he stared down at the wetness of her tears on his fingertips and briefly closed his eyes as a great wave of relief washed over him. 'It's okay,' he said, but his voice was rough with emotion.

In the morning the doctor visited and examined Alexius, straightening up with a broad smile. 'That's the great thing about babies,' he said cheerfully. 'They worry the life out of you and then they bounce right back.'

Once he had gone, Xandros turned to her, his features shuttered, for the fear of what could have been was eating him up inside. 'I am hiring two nursery nurses to sit with both babies at night,' he announced.

'But I want to look after them myself,' she whispered.

'Rebecca, I am not listening to any kind of argument—so you can wipe that stubborn look off your face.' His face darkened, his accent growing more pronounced. 'You cannot—and I mean that *literally*—sit up with your children day and night. You will collapse from exhaustion—and what good will that do anyone? Tell me that!'

She couldn't fault his logic, but she felt as though everything was slipping from beyond her control. Hadn't she been learning how to cope with their twins—and now this?

For the next few days, she operated on autopilot—drawing on reserves of energy and strength she didn't know she possessed. The night-nurses were caring and efficient and as the days passed it was clear that Alexius was better in every way and that Andreas wasn't affected, but Rebecca didn't seem able to convince herself of that. It was like living in a recurring nightmare.

On the hour, every hour she awoke during the night with some superstitious fear making her sit bolt upright in bed, as if something awful were about to happen. She would rush into the nursery to find the nurses watching over her two angels and they would look at her as if she were very slightly…well, mad.

Until the afternoon the doctor visited and he and Xandros confronted her in the sitting room.

'Sit down,' commanded Xandros sternly.

'But—'

'I said, sit *down*.'

She sank onto one of the sofas and looked up at the two men—at the dark and obdurate expression glittering from Xandros's black eyes.

'Rebecca, you've got to slow down,' said the doctor quietly. 'You won't be good to either baby if you wear yourself out.'

'I'm trying.'

He shook his head. 'No more haunting the nursery at night. Only get up when you need to feed them. Sleep deprivation is a form of torture you know. You need to sleep.'

'But I can't sleep, Doctor.'

'Why not?' he questioned.

'Because…' She shrugged her shoulders, aware that Xandros was studying her as if she were a specimen in a test-tube. And didn't she feel a bit like that herself? Like some strange species which defied definition? 'I don't know,' she whispered.

'You should be focussing your attention on your partner a little more,' continued the doctor, warming to what was obviously a well-worn post-pregnancy theme, and Rebecca felt her cheeks grow pink with embarrassment.

Didn't he realise that her relationship with Xandros

was not a relationship at all? That they were parents, but nothing more intimate than that? No, of course he didn't.

'Thank you, Doctor,' she said stiffly.

The medic turned to Xandros. 'And you'll make sure she rests?'

Xandros gave a grim kind of smile. 'Oh, yes, Doctor—you can be assured of that.'

That evening, after the twins had been fed and bathed and put to bed, Xandros made Rebecca sit down and eat the meal which Betty had prepared and left for them in the dining room.

'Now drink a glass of wine,' he said. 'One won't hurt you.'

Obediently, she drank some. 'How's that?'

'Good. Now eat your dinner.'

The wine had begun to relax her. How long since she had properly relaxed? How long since she had wanted to? 'Will I get a gold star if I do?' she questioned flippantly.

'We'll see.' He drank some wine himself, his eyes shuttered. He thought about the night of the party and the way she had been in his arms. Had she forgotten about that? Or put it out of her mind because it made her feel guilty—or simply because she had recognised that sex would only complicate an already complicated relationship?

That kiss had been fuelled by anger and jealousy—it was easy to kiss a woman on those terms—but maybe it was not fair to do that in Rebecca's case. Not now. Not after all that had happened between them. Xandros didn't doubt for a moment that he could make her want him—but wouldn't that provide only a quick fix?

After dinner and after she'd insisted on checking on the twins one more time and met the calm, indulgent smiles of the two nurses, he walked with her to her bedroom. If he hadn't ached for her quite so much, it might have amused him to be playing so chivalrous a role for the first time in his life.

'Goodnight, Rebecca,' he said softly.

And suddenly the old fears were back. She swallowed—staring up into his beautiful shadowed face. How approachable he had been tonight, she thought, her heart aching. As if she could tell him anything. What would he say if she told him she still loved him? Would his accessible air desert him, to be replaced by that flinty and cool expression which used to set her nerves on edge? 'Goodnight, Xandros,' she whispered.

She undressed and slipped on a nightgown—for she never slept naked since giving birth—and then she extinguished the lights and climbed into bed. But even after the wine and the doctor's reassurances and the knowledge that her children were being well cared for, sleep refused to come. She lay there, switching from one side to the other, turning the pillow so that its cool side touched her hot cheek. Until she became aware of the shaft of light from the door which had quietly opened, and the tall and shadowy form of Xandros standing in the threshold, and, turning her head to stare at him, she felt her heart give a painful kind of lurch.

She sat up in bed. 'Is something wrong?'

'No, nothing is wrong,' he said, walking into the

darkened room. 'I've been working and came by to check whether you were asleep, But I see for myself that you're not.'

'No, I can't.' She stared hopefully at the faint light which gleamed from his ebony eyes—as if he would be able to wave a magic wand and take away some of her tension. For the night-time could be the scariest and loneliest place in the world. She swallowed—for surely it was no sin to long for a little human company. 'Stay for a bit,' she said. 'Stay and keep me company for a while.'

He could read from her body language that she was not intending to be predatory—he had never met a woman less predatory than Rebecca—and yet her innocent request was a barbed one. Did she realise what she was asking of him?

He knew that women could kill their desire in a way which men found excruciatingly difficult—but he could hear the fear in her voice and he sat down on the edge of the bed, aware of her soft warmth within touching distance, and expelled a ragged breath. This was going to be torture, he realised.

'Now what are we going to do?' he questioned, but she didn't seem to pick up on the irony of his question.

'Talk to me.' She wriggled into the mattress. 'Tell me about your brother and why you don't speak any more.'

In the darkness, he gave a wry smile. If anything was designed to kill desire, it was concentrating on old feuds and old scores. He hadn't thought of it for years—or maybe he just hadn't let himself. Sometimes things happened and you simply accepted them, without asking yourself why.

'It was male rivalry,' he said slowly, realising that he was able to look at it dispassionately for perhaps the first time in his life. Was that with the benefit of hindsight—time and distance making things seem more understandable? Or was it just the way Rebecca had of asking—as if she wanted to know for reasons which mattered, rather than acquiring knowledge which she could one day use against him?

'We lived on an island which was too small for two big personalities and we had a family business—which needed only one son to run it. It was a fight to see which of us would win control—like we had fought for everything all our lives.'

A fight he had grown bored with—and was glad that he had done so, he realised suddenly. For now he recognised that Kalfera would have swallowed him up—and that his character was much better suited to a life outside. He liked cities—creating them and living in them.

Rebecca turned her head to look at his shadowed profile. 'I hope that our boys don't fall out when they're older.'

'That's out of our hands,' he said softly and he reached out to touch her silken hair. 'Go to sleep now, Rebecca.'

'Mmm.' She felt her eyelids growing heavy, as sleepy as if someone had slipped her a narcotic. Was it the absence of fear, the glass of wine—or because Xandros was now stroking her hair in that reassuring and rhythmical way which made her feel so safe and secure?

'That's nice,' she murmured.

'Is it?' he questioned thickly. Was he *crazy*? Or was she being a little less innocent than he thought?

'Mmm.' Instinctively, she wriggled towards him, colliding with the warmth of his body. So was that. Oh, heavens—how could she have forgotten how good he felt? And smelt. And tasted.

'Rebecca?'

'Mmm?'

'Go to sleep.'

'If I go to sleep, then you'll leave.'

There was a pause. 'If I stay, you may get more than you bargained for,' he said softly.

Her eyes opened and she looked up at him. He was close. So close. Her heart turned over. 'Like what?'

'Like this.' Reaching out, he touched his fingertip to her lips, tracing around their curved bow with a brush so light it was barely there and hearing her instinctive intake of breath.

She released the breath in a low, shaking rush. 'But I like that.'

'Do you?'

'Mmm.'

'And what else?' He began to stroke the silken skin of her neck—a whisper of a touch which made her shiver beneath him. 'What else do you like, Rebecca?'

Her heart was hammering like violent rain on a rooftop. 'Kisses,' she managed.

'Ah, kisses.' Kisses were different, he realised as he moved next to her on the bed and lowered his mouth to hers—or, rather, this one was. Slow and drugging, sensual and yet almost innocent—it felt like kissing someone for the first time. Except that he could never remember it being like this before. Not with anyone. As if he were drowning in a sweetness so intense it made him want to cry out.

He felt her move even closer to him and now she was threading her fingers luxuriously in his hair. And suddenly he was cupping her face with his hands and staring down into her wide, darkened eyes and her parted lips. 'Rebecca,' he said simply. It was a question asked and answered in that one, simple word.

She began to unbutton his shirt, touching her lips to his chest and sliding the fine silk away from the broad shoulders. He groaned as she began to unbuckle his belt, her fingertips skating lightly over his hardness, and in that moment he felt all self-restraint slip away as she began to edge his jeans down.

With a little moan of pleasure, he peeled the night-gown from her, and then they were both naked—and never had this intimacy felt quite so intense. The silken feel of her warm skin beneath his fingers was like a glorious homecoming and a discovery all at once. Her hands were trembling—and so was her body as he began to explore the soft contours of her shape. Her new, womanly shape. This mother of his children.

He wanted to make it last for ever and yet he wanted it to be over in an instant to relieve him of this feeling which was threatening to engulf him—to swamp him with feelings surely better kept at bay—and suddenly he moved over her, knowing that he could wait no more.

'Xandros!' He had lulled her with his soft words and unfamiliar tenderness, but the shock of him entering her body after so long was like something

else. Like finding sweet water in the middle of an unforgiving desert, and it made her cry out in joyful yet
pained recognition that—like the desert's water—this
was all an illusion.

He stilled. 'I am hurting you?'

'No!' Or, at least, not in the way he meant—for her
body could always accommodate this proud, virile
Greek, even if her heart was made of less resilient
stuff. 'No, you're not hurting me, Xandros.'

'Ah!' His lips were on her breasts and in her hair.
They whispered along her neck and over the scented
hollows of her shoulders. Moving slowly, with each
perfect thrust he increased the pleasure, notch by
notch. She moved beneath him—moving with
growing and impatient pleasure. Until at last she gave
the beginnings of a low, soft moan which he kissed
quiet—aware that the house was not empty. And only
then did he spill out his seed with one long and shuddering breath of release.

Afterwards, he fell asleep easily—as he always had
done after sex, the same and yet surely not the same
at all. Rebecca thought that this moment should have
felt like some kind of immense victory—so why did
it feel so curiously empty?

She stared up at the ceiling as the slow, steady
rhythm of Xandros's breathing warmed her neck. And
the questions which had been put on hold for so long
now came rushing into her mind, demanding answers.

CHAPTER TWELVE

It was past dawn when Xandros awoke, narrowing his eyes against the pale light filtering in through the windows—his surroundings as unfamiliar as the sweet saturation of his senses.

He was in Rebecca's bed!

He turned his head to look for her, but his first instinct had been the right one, he realised. He was alone—the rumpled sheets and the faint, musky scent of sex were the only signs that he had not dreamt up the mind-blowing love-making they had indulged in last night.

So where was she? He yawned. With the babies?

Automatically, his mouth curved into a smile and he raised his arms up above his head and stretched, lazily, before getting out of bed and pulling on his discarded jeans and loosely buttoning his shirt. He would go and look for her. Bring her back to bed.

He found her downstairs in the kitchen—her back to him as she stood staring out into the deserted, dawn-fresh street. She must have just fed the twins, for she was drinking thirstily from a large glass of water and she did not appear to hear him enter the room.

'Rebecca?' he said softly.

Unseen, Rebecca's fingers tightened around the glass—as if she could extract some kind of courage from its cool, smooth surface. But she didn't say anything. Not yet. No. She didn't trust herself.

He took her silence for shyness. Of course she would be shy—after what had happened between them. It had been…amazing. His bare feet soundless on the tiled floor, he walked over to her and bent his face to her neck, inhaling her sweet scent as he revelled in the silken feel of her hair against his skin.

'Come back to bed,' he murmured, aware of the growing ache at his groin.

She stiffened. 'I'm not tired.'

'Perfect.' His voice dipped. 'Neither am I.'

But Rebecca's shoulders remained stiff—her body as straight and unforgiving as a sentry—determined not to relax by even a fraction for Xandros was much too powerful. One touch and she would weaken and her resolve would be lost.

'I think I'll go and have a shower and get dressed,' she said.

Now that most definitely did not sound as if she was extending a sensual invitation. Xandros narrowed his eyes. 'Rebecca?'

She knew that she could not carry on standing staring out of the window, that she needed to face him, but it was the hardest thing she could remember doing in a long time—wiping all the emotion and longing from her face so that he would not be able to seize on any vulnerability. Because she was not going to *do* vulnerable any more. What she was about to do next was the only possible way forward.

Turning round, she gave him the kind of quick, polite smile she might have used if he were back in one of the passenger seats at Evolo airlines—and she were about to offer him a cup of coffee.

'It's not worth going back to bed,' she said briskly.

He gave her one last chance. Maybe this was decorum speaking. A woman seeking approval after such an abandoned response in his arms. He could go along with that. 'Rebecca,' he said softly. *'Agape mou.'*

It should have been enough. There was a whole world of sensual promise in those words, the soft and faintly accented way he said her name, which was incomparable to the way that any other mortal said it. And maybe in any other circumstances it would have been enough—for it would have been easy to have slipped into his warm embrace. Much, much too easy to have given herself up to his seeking kiss. To have allowed him to lead her upstairs, not saying anything for fear of disturbing their children or their nurses— but trying to hide their secret, complicit smiles while inside their hearts were bursting with the excitement of what was about to take place.

But Xandros's *heart* would not be bursting, she reminded herself. The source of *his* excitement was seated in a place far more elemental—and *that* was what she needed to remember. Not *her* wishes, or dreams or hopes or foolish longings that one day he might love her with the same passion which burned so brightly in her heart for him. Because he wouldn't.

Xandros didn't *do* love—not the adult kind between

man and woman—he'd never pretended to. He loved his babies and that was growing day by day—but there was never going to be anything deeper left over for her. And maybe she shouldn't expect there to be—for he'd never made any promises to her, had he? So he wasn't breaking any. Surely it wasn't fair to blame *him* for falling short of *her* expectations.

Yet if they carried on deepening the relationship through sex then she would be lost—she knew that for sure, because that was what happened to women. They used sex as an expression of their love in a way that men didn't need to and sometimes they got hurt. And if she did that she wasn't simply putting herself at risk—but the whole steady emotional landscape which the twins needed. More than needed.

So could she do it—deny what she most craved? Xandros in her arms every night—bringing her the pleasure which only he could? It was tempting. Of course it was. But it was also dangerous. Surely too dangerous to even contemplate?

If she allowed their physical relationship to resume—then wasn't she placing herself in jeopardy of that old, needy Rebecca returning? The one who used to tiptoe around him trying to gauge what his mood was. Because there was no room in her life for someone like that any more. It had been glaringly obvious that when she had done that he'd lost respect for her—hell, she'd lost respect for *herself*—so why would any sane person elect to go right back there?

The alternative was pretending. That the sex was just sex and that she didn't love him. Pretending to be flippant and pretending that she didn't care. But she did. Of course she did. She had never stopped loving him, not really—and she was damned if she was going to live a lie. What kind of example would she be setting to Andreas and Alexius if she did?

So tell him. Don't play stupid games. Xandros is an intelligent man and he'll accept what you say. He'll have to.

'Last night…'

'Ah, *ne*—last night,' he echoed huskily. 'Last night.'

Somehow she kept her smile. Not too wide and slightly impersonal, she thought—because she didn't want them to fall out. This wasn't a feud, after all, but a practical solution to a troublesome area of their lives. 'Was a mistake,' she said.

Xandros narrowed his eyes. 'A *mistake*?'

'And one which must not be repeated,' she forged on—as if forcing herself to chew a whole mouthful of poison before swallowing it. 'Xandros, we can't carry on sleeping together.'

His first flippant thought was to murmur that he didn't intend to do much sleeping, because he didn't think for a moment that she meant it. Women never refused him—and Rebecca had always been like soft putty within his experienced fingers. But something in her violet eyes warned him that this was different. That she *did* mean it.

His mouth hardened.

She could *not* mean it!

Desire urged him to place his hand on her bare arm—knowing that just a simple touch should ensure that she would dissolve beneath it—but a far fiercer streak of pride stopped him. Did she think that he would beg? *He? Beg?* His mouth curved into a cruel smile. Why, let him withdraw and then let her see how long she could sustain her opposition to what they both wanted. Soon she would be begging *him* to take her once more!

But as the days passed Xandros discovered that Rebecca did not beg—and neither did she sulk—and he found himself caught up in an unfamiliar cloud of confusion. She was perfectly polite and sweet. She continued to be an exemplary mother. She even had intelligent observations to make about the international news. If he had been interviewing her for a job, he would have found himself highly impressed—but he was not interviewing her for a job. He wanted her back in his bed! And he wanted her now!

'Rebecca,' he growled, over breakfast one morning—before his trip to the Greek Embassy, where he had promised the Ambassador that he would consider designing a new library for the building.

Rebecca glanced up from her yoghurt, steeling herself to look at him. He was wearing a creamy linen suit and tiny droplets of water sparkled like jewels in the depths of the ebony hair. His skin glowed golden-olive with life and vitality and she thought that she had never seen him look quite so vibrant. Or so gorgeous.

'Yes, Xandros?'

'This cannot go on!'

She pushed the yoghurt away. 'What can't?'

'Do not play the innocent with me, my beauty!' He slammed his coffee-cup down and the delicate white china seemed to shimmer dangerously in its saucer. 'Or perhaps that is your sport? To play games with me? To see how exquisitely you can increase my desire for you?'

Rebecca swallowed. Her fingers were shaking and she prayed he would not see—because she needed to be strong in her resolve. She *needed* to. 'I'm not playing games with you, Xandros,' she said truthfully. 'I told you how I believed our relationship would best endure and my stance on that has not changed.' She shrugged. 'I'm sorry.'

He wanted to slam his fist on the table—to tell her that she was *not* sorry! Or that she had no need to be sorry when the situation could be so sweetly reversed at any given time. But he saw her calm and unswerving gaze and realised with an already heavy heart that she meant it.

All day, thoughts of her obsessed him—in a way which was completely alien to him. Several times he had to ask the Ambassador to repeat himself and he was completely indifferent to the way that the First Secretary kept crossing and uncrossing her legs—showing a very obvious glimpse of bare flesh above the silk of her stocking top. In fact, his mouth curved in such obvious distaste that he was pleased to see her tugging at the hem of her skirt in response.

That night he had dinner with a friend who was over from New York, but he remained distracted throughout the meal. He had wondered whether Rebecca might quiz him about his whereabouts when he arrived home, but to his surprise, and then to his fury, she did not.

Moodily, he went and found her in the nursery, sitting chatting quite happily with one of the nurses and smiling widely at him when he walked in with a face as dark as thunder—which only dispersed when he picked up Andreas and held him close.

And as he met a steady pair of violet eyes over the top of the baby's silken head he recognised that retreating from her would not work—and a cold fear began to clamp its icy fingers around him. *Fear!* Yes, fear—real and present. For Xandros a strange and unwelcome sensation and yet one which he was discovering was shockingly recognisable from a past he had buried for much too long.

For the next two nights he did not sleep more than thirty minutes at a stretch—several times rising from his bed to go in search of her. And every time he halted, his hand falling away from the door handle to clench beside the taut, tense shaft of his thigh. Recognising that it would be wrong to try to use the cloak of darkness to conceal the turmoil in his mind. Or to seduce her when her body was soft and receptive with sleep.

He sat working in his studio while he chose his moment with all the precision and care for which he was renowned in his professional life. The two daytime nannies he'd insisted on employing to give Rebecca an occasional break decided to capitalise on an unexpected spell of sunshine by taking the boys for a stroll in their prams.

Xandros watched them walking side by side down the tree-lined road and then he went to find Rebecca— his breath hot and tight in his throat as he made his way to the smaller of the two drawing rooms. She was gluing photos into an old-fashioned baby book, but she stopped what she was doing when he walked in.

'H-hello, Xandros,' she said hesitantly, because his face was dark with a look on it she had never seen before and she felt her heart begin to race—for was this not what she had most dreaded and expected? That he was about to tell her he couldn't continue in such a situation. That he was off to find a woman who would welcome him with warm and open arms. Unless he had already found someone! The racing of her heart continued so fast that it felt like something close to pain. 'What can I do for you?'

There was a pause. 'I cannot go on like this!'

Her vision swam, her fingers clutching at the desk. 'You can't?' She nodded. 'No, of course you can't.'

'No man of flesh and blood could endure it,' he breathed, flicking his gaze over her—at her slim, strong body clad in a simple white dress and wondering what she wore beneath. 'And that is why I am offering you your freedom.'

It was everything she had feared, and more. 'My freedom,' she repeated painfully.

Xandros nodded. 'I will sign this house over to you,' he said. 'Or buy you an alternative property if that is what you would prefer. I will also set up a lifetime payment and settlement for you—so you can bring the boys up without fear of financial insecurity.' His mouth tightened. 'It will, of course, be a generous settlement.'

'Of course,' said Rebecca weakly and once again she hesitated. 'And what precisely would you want in return for this generosity?'

Black eyes narrowed into glittering shards of jet. 'I want shared access to the twins and arrangements set in place to ensure that they can travel between England and America. While they are with me, you will of course have all the freedom at your disposal to pursue other relationships, should you wish.'

The sinking feeling inside her increased. 'And does this "offer" come with any conditions, Xandros?'

'Indeed it does.' His mouth grew hard. 'That you do not bring another man into the home of my sons—on either a temporary or a permanent basis. If you do that, then I shall seek custody.'

'I see.' She sucked in a breath. 'And that's what you want, is it?'

He stared at her. How emotionless she sounded! How matter-of-fact her question! Could this really be the same woman who had wept with pleasure countless times in his arms? Who had carried his children beneath her heart? And, suddenly, he no longer wanted to make it easy for her. He wanted—no, needed—to show her how he really felt. Could he? Dared he?

When his mother had left the family for another man the other children on the island had whispered about the scandal. But he and Kyros had never admitted—not even to each other—how much the gossip as well as her betrayal had wounded them. Hurt pride had only added to their sense of desertion. That was why they had retreated inside themselves, he saw that now quite clearly. Hiding their emotions from the world—and from themselves until they had been convinced that they had been washed clean of all emotion.

And suddenly he saw that now he risked losing everything in his futile attempt to protect himself from similar pain. That life *was* painful. That pain was simply the reverse side of pleasure—and you could not have or appreciate one without the other. Which meant he had to risk that kind of hurt happening all over again.

'No, of course it's not what I want!' he ground out. '*You* are what I want, Rebecca—you and only you, to be my partner in the fullest sense of the word.'

There was a long pause while she stared at him. 'But why should you want that?' she persisted—aware that the ravaged hurt on his face must now be reflected on her own. 'Because you are missing sex?'

'Not because of *sex*! I can have sex whenever I click my fingers!' he roared, outraged. 'Because I love you, of course. I have grown to love you,' he said simply, a note of surprise deepening his voice as his black eyes burned into her. 'So do you want your freedom or not, Rebecca—because you know that there is always another option.'

She stared at him, scarcely able to breathe, for fear that she would disturb the strange kind of magic his unexpected words of love had brought glimmering into the atmosphere. 'What option is that?' she whispered.

His gaze was intense. 'The other option is my heart.' He seemed to dominate the room with his height and the sheer force of his personality. 'Take it, for you alone have unlocked it—and now it is yours to keep.' His voice softened. 'If you want it.'

Tears began to prick at her eyes, but she forced herself to blink them away. She shook her head. 'Of course I want it! But you don't mean that, Xandros,' she whispered. 'You can't.'

'Can't I?' He walked over to where she was sitting and pulled her to her feet. 'Yes, I mean it—every word of it and more. What a fool I have been not to have realised it sooner. I want *you*, my love. My brave, sweet Rebecca. My only love.' He stared down into her beautiful face, seeing the bright tears now in her eyes. 'Do not cry, *agape mou*. Please do not cry—for your Xandros forbids it.'

Yet she could not stop—nor wanted to stop—the tears which trickled down her cheeks, recognising these were tears of joy and dazed disbelief, not tears of sorrow.

He dried them away with his fingertips as once he had done before—when their sick baby had begun to breathe properly—and then cupped her face tenderly within the palms of his hands. She was trembling as she stared up at him, knowing that, just as Xandros had offered her his heart, he had carved a place in her own a long time ago—a place so deep that no force on earth could ever remove him from it.

And as he pulled her close she suddenly understood that she would never have to doubt the commitment of his words to her. Because here was a man who had never made her false promises, who would not say something unless he meant it—he would have no cause to.

'Will you kiss me now?' she whispered breathlessly.

'*Will* I?' He looked down at her for one long moment, his face filled with love and a wild kind of exultation. 'Just try and stop me, *agape mou*.'

EPILOGUE

'SO DO you think he enjoyed himself?'

Xandros heard the faint anxiety in Rebecca's voice as she turned away from the snowy window.

'Of course he did. He loved it,' he said softly. 'He adored you and was completely smitten by the twins.' Xandros paused, for he had never seen his father look quite so contented. 'He is a proud grandfather.'

'Yes,' said Rebecca. Though it must have brought back all kinds of bitter-sweet memories for Xandros's father to see the two babies. History repeating itself, in a way—though not in every way. She would make sure of that—because she wasn't planning on going anywhere. She gazed over at her Greek lover and her lips softened with love.

She and Xandros had moved to New York when the twins were six months old and bought a brownstone in a wonderful district called Gramercy Park, which Rebecca couldn't quite believe existed. It was planted with trees—willow, chestnut and elm—and their garden was full of roses and lilac. It was an amazing neighbourhood—a green oasis in a fast-moving city which Rebecca was quickly learning to know, and love.

Xandros had employed an award-winning architect to work in his company so that he could cut back himself. He occupied himself with enough projects to keep his creative ambition flowing—but which left him enough time to see his wonderful sons blossom and grow.

She stared at him now—at his beloved, dark and autocratic profile. He was opening a bottle of champagne and he turned his head to look at her.

'What?' he said, meeting the silent question in her eyes.

Rebecca had learnt much about this man she loved. That in the past he had been emotionally defensive in order to protect himself from the pain which was a legacy from his own childhood. But she had also learnt that you couldn't keep running away from stuff simply because it made you feel uncomfortable—that the only way to overcome it was to face it head-on, and she hoped that Xandros was learning that, too. 'I wondered if I was ever going to get to meet your twin brother,' she said quietly.

A smile curved his lips. Had she read his thoughts? he wondered. 'I was planning to speak to you about that.' He handed her a glass of champagne.

'Are we celebrating something?'

'Mmm?' He lifted his black brows and gave a lazy smile. 'But of course. Our life is one long celebration, is it not, *agape mou*?' he questioned softly.

'Oh, Xandros,' she murmured, biting her lip with pleasure. 'That's so corny.'

'But true.'

'Well, yes.'

'So will you please marry me, Rebecca?'

'*Marry* you?' She put her glass down quickly, afraid of dropping it with fingers which were suddenly shaky. 'Why?'

'Why?' He shook his head. She never ceased to surprise him. Who would have thought that one of New York's most eligible bachelors would have had his marriage proposal treated with such cool analysis? 'Why do you think?'

Forcing herself to be pragmatic, Rebecca shrugged. 'Because it makes getting a visa easier?' She saw his face darken. 'To regularise matters for the boys' sake?'

Xandros put his own glass down. 'I cannot believe that I am hearing this! You disregard the most important reason of all for getting married?' he demanded. 'What about love? Because we happen to love one another—isn't that the only valid reason for asking you to be my wife?'

Rebecca sucked in a deep breath. Maybe this was meant to be. A chance to free herself of something which had been troubling her—not in a big way, but occasionally rearing its persistent head to nag at her. 'But we're only together because of the twins, aren't we?' she pointed out falteringly. 'I mean, I know we love each other now—but if I hadn't got pregnant then we would still be apart. And sometimes I wonder— well, worry, actually—whether you regret or resent the fact that you were kind of…trapped into this.'

Xandros did not answer straight away. Always the most articulate of men in both languages, he knew

that what he said now was of the utmost importance—
so that the subject could be discussed and then put
aside for ever. In the past, where all the heartache
belonged.

'This much is true,' he admitted, seeing her rose-
petal mouth pucker. 'Perhaps it would have pleased us
both more if we had simply met and fallen in love. But
we have come through much to attain the happiness
we have today, Rebecca—and something hard-fought
for is more precious than anything. Because life does
not always follow rules, *agape mou*. Sometimes you
have to make up your own in order to create your own
fairy tale—and that is more satisfactory. Much more.'
His black eyes gleamed with love as her lips began to
curve into a smile. 'And you still haven't answered my
question. Will you marry me?'

And Rebecca began to smile as she ran across the
room towards him and flung her arms around his neck.
'Of course I'll marry you, my beloved, darling
Xandros.'

As he held her tight Rebecca thought that maybe his
twin brother would come to their wedding and she
would get to meet him at last. And maybe he and
Xandros would bury the hatchet and make their peace.
Xandros was right. You could make your own fairy tale
happen—and the possibilities were endless.

Best of all, theirs was only just beginning.

Celebrate 100 years of pure reading pleasure with Mills & Boon®

To mark our centenary, each month we're publishing a special 100th Birthday Edition. These celebratory editions are packed with extra features and include a FREE bonus story.

Plus, starting in February you'll have the chance to enter a fabulous monthly prize draw. See 100th Birthday Edition books for details.

Now that's worth celebrating!

15th February 2008

Raintree: Inferno by Linda Howard
Includes FREE bonus story Loving Evangeline
A double dose of Linda Howard's heady mix of passion and adventure

4th April 2008

The Guardian's Forbidden Mistress by Miranda Lee
Includes FREE bonus story The Magnate's Mistress
Two glamorous and sensual reads from favourite author Miranda Lee!

2nd May 2008

The Last Rake in London by Nicola Cornick
Includes FREE bonus story The Notorious Lord
Lose yourself in two tales of high society and rakish seduction!

Look for Mills & Boon 100th Birthday Editions at your favourite bookseller or visit
www.millsandboon.co.uk

FREE

4 BOOKS AND A SURPRISE GIFT!

We would like to take this opportunity to thank you for reading this Mills & Boon® book by offering you the chance to take FOUR more specially selected titles from the Modern™ series absolutely FREE! We're also making this offer to introduce you to the benefits of the Mills & Boon® Reader Service™—

- ★ **FREE home delivery**
- ★ **FREE gifts and competitions**
- ★ **FREE monthly Newsletter**
- ★ **Books available before they're in the shops**
- ★ **Exclusive Reader Service offers**

Accepting these FREE books and gift places you under no obligation to buy; you may cancel at any time, even after receiving your free shipment. Simply complete your details below and return the entire page to the address below. You don't even need a stamp!

YES! Please send me 4 free Modern books and a surprise gift. I understand that unless you hear from me, I will receive 6 superb new titles every month for just £2.99 each, postage and packing free. I am under no obligation to purchase any books and may cancel my subscription at any time. The free books and gift will be mine to keep in any case.

P8ZEE

Ms/Mrs/Miss/Mr...Initials ....
BLOCK CAPITALS PLEASE

Surname ....

Address ....

....

....Postcode ....

Send this whole page to:

The Reader Service, FREEPOST CN81, Croydon, CR9 3WZ